SHADOW OF THE SASQUATCH

J.H. MONCRIEFF

SEVERED PRESS
HOBART TASMANIA

SHADOW OF THE SASQUATCH

ISBN: 978-1-922551-65-8

For Nicole Burch, with thanks and gratitude

PROLOGUE

For Riley Tanner, it was the house dreams were made of. When the real estate agent guided his Hummer up the winding driveway and she got her first glimpse of the wooden A-frame, constructed of logs and tucked into the Oregon wilderness that surrounded it, Riley's designer mind began working overtime. Though it needed a little TLC, the potential was immediately apparent. Before she could reign herself in, she was imagining a covered deck, perfect for hosting family barbecues, and a little studio with floor-to-ceiling windows, where she could work as she watched the birds.

She socked the agent on the arm. Hard.

"Ouch! What was that for?" Rod assumed a wounded expression that made her want to hit him again. This time, he dodged her.

"You evil, horrible, terrible man. How could you bring me here?"

"But—I thought you'd love it. You said you wanted something away from the city, something quiet. It's hard to get quieter than this."

"That's the problem. It's perfect. It has to be what, though—" She squinted up at the house, considering. "A three bedroom? You know that's way out of our price range. Showing this to me is akin to torture."

Rod grinned, displaying the gold-capped front tooth that never failed to startle her. *You're a real estate agent, not a rapper*, she was always tempted to say. Thus far, she'd managed to hold back. At least he was on their side—or she'd thought he was. Until now. "Four bedrooms. And three baths. Three *full* baths."

Three full baths? Four bedrooms? It was too much space for the three of them, and yet, Riley's mind raced ahead, imagining Brooke having her choice of rooms. A real guestroom for overnight visitors instead of a pullout couch in the basement. Or perhaps an office. Maybe both? She could get one of those contraptions that was a desk during the day and a bed at night.

The memory of that day's bank balance brought her crashing back to earth. "It's too much. We'd never be able to afford it."

Rod's grin didn't fade as he scribbled an impossibly low number on a piece of paper and handed it to her. "And the best part is, the owners are highly motivated."

Rather than weep for joy at this good fortune, Riley raised an eyebrow. "What's the catch?"

"Catch? What catch? There is no catch." But the agent wouldn't meet her eyes.

"C'mon, Rod—I wasn't born yesterday. No one sells a four-bedroom house for this price; I don't care how bad the economy is. What's the story? Did someone die here?"

For this kind of luxury, putting up with ghosts would be worth it.

He laughed, but there was something false sounding about it, something she didn't like. "Of course not. I think they found the place too isolating. They're eager to get back to the city and be done with what turned out to be a failed experiment with country living. Besides, you haven't seen the inside yet. You might hate it."

"I doubt that." Riley opened the Hummer's door and jumped to the ground, excited to explore the most perfect house she'd ever seen. It ticked all of her boxes, and some of Jason's too. But that nagging, pesky, logical part of her kept whispering that this was too good to be true. "You promise it's not sitting on an ancient Indian burial ground? No poltergeists?"

Raising a hand, he placed the other over his heart. "Scout's honor. There's nothing wrong with the house, I promise."

She doubted the greasy bastard had ever been a Scout, but the house's lure was too strong for her to argue. As Rod fumbled with the lock, Riley shifted her weight from foot to foot, unable to bear any further delays.

The house smelled of cedar and wood smoke, strong scent memories from her childhood. The afternoon sun cast a golden glow on the wooden floor planks, and she paused in wonder, resting her hand on the doorknob. It was beautiful, more lovely than she could have imagined. Jason was the one with an eye for how things were built, but as far as she could tell, the place had been completely refurbished. Clicking a switch, Rod set a ceiling fan into motion, ruffling her hair in its breeze.

With every room, she fell more in love. The old-fashioned AGA range in the kitchen. The peaked ceilings in the upstairs bedrooms. The pedestal sinks and clawfoot tubs. The house was worth at least three times what the owners were asking, if not more. She couldn't wrap her head around it. As she struggled to make sense of it, Rod blathered on.

"One downside—there isn't a garage. Yet. They planned to build one but hadn't gotten around to it. There's a shed. We can go see that next, if you like."

"Rod, you have to level with me. I can see how much went into this place; why would they sell for so low? No matter how eager they are to move back to the city, they could get so much more. This doesn't make any sense."

He shrugged. "Who am I to question their decision? My job is to get the best price for *you*."

"I love this house; you know I do. But there has to be something wrong with it, and I'd rather know now. Whatever it is, we can probably deal with it, just please be honest. Is it a cracked foundation? Old plumbing?" She'd thrown that last one in for the heck of it. She'd already seen the pipes were copper, shiny and new.

"Riley, I swear on my mother's grave. There is nothing wrong with this house."

Once again, that subtle emphasis on the word *house*. "Is it the property, then? Is it on a floodplain? Some multimillionaire investor has a lien on it? What?"

"No, nothing like that." He waved his hand in the air, as though dismissing her. Too bad he'd moved out of range.

"But there *is* something."

"Not really. Not for you, I wouldn't say."

"What's that supposed to mean?" She was mortified to feel the sting of tears, but the thought of all those gorgeous dreams dying before they had a chance to become reality was agonizing.

"They're city people. You grew up in the country. You know how it is."

"What, exactly, are we talking about? Spit it out—I can take it."

"I don't know many details. They didn't give me a lot to go on. I heard a few things about the lady of the house being frightened by night noises."

"Night noises?"

"Animals, wildlife, stuff like that. Nothing that would bother you, but when you're from the city, an owl fart is probably terrifying." He laughed again, and it still sounded fake. She wasn't amused. Why did dudes always have to blame the woman? If they were selling at that cut-rate a price, the husband had to have agreed as well.

"And that's all it was?"

"Yes, I swear." He repeated his half-assed Scout salute, attempting to look sincere. It sounded off—she didn't want to guess how much money the owners would lose by selling at that price—but Riley wanted to be convinced. She didn't scare easily, and neither did Jason. They were both good shots. If some animal had picked this place to terrorize, she was confident they could handle it. No bear, wolf, or badger was going to keep her from her dream home.

Rod cleared his throat. "If you're interested, I wouldn't wait too long. At this price, there have been a lot of inquiries."

"We'll take it," Riley said, crossing her fingers that Jason would forgive her.

CHAPTER ONE

Three months later.

"Have you considered returning to work?"

Nat McPherson gazed at the therapist through smudged sunglasses. "Have you considered not charging for your lame-ass advice?"

To her disappointment, Kathy didn't appear the slightest bit offended. "Getting back into a routine would be good for you. Besides, you love what you do. I hate to use a cliché, but going back to podcasting might give you a new lease on life."

Nat rolled her eyes, the expression wasted behind the dark lenses. "You always use clichés."

"Only because I know how much you adore them. What do you say? What's the worst that could happen?"

That was enough to make Nat slip the sunglasses down an inch to glare at her. "You didn't just ask me that. My *job* is the reason my best friend was brutally murdered. My *job* is the reason several other good people are dead. My *job* is the reason I spent months in a Russian prison, waiting to be extradited. Please tell me you're not that stupid."

"The problem is, you don't blame your job. You blame yourself."

The glasses went back up as Nat's eyes watered. Damn straight she blamed herself. If she hadn't let that troll goad her into dragging Andrew to Dyatlov Pass, her friend would still be alive. And she'd still be a contributing member of society, as much as she ever was.

"Potato, potatah." Nat crossed her arms. "I'm not going back."

"You told me yourself that you'd stopped going on excursions long before Dyatlov. As long as you host your podcast from the comfort of your own studio, you'll be fine. And I think it will be good for you. You have to do something, Nat. Speaking as your friend, not your therapist, you're a mess."

"It's a good thing you used that disclaimer. Saying I'm a mess isn't exactly therapeutic."

"How much have you had to drink today?" Kathy shot back.

"Nothing...not much, I mean. Maybe half a glass. Hardly anything." Besides, the vodka here paled in comparison to Igor's cherished stash. Maybe it was time to pay him a visit. She'd heard he was in even worse shape. Would the Russian government let her back in the country?

"Bullshit. Behind those glasses, I'm willing to bet your eyes are crimson. Those clothes look like they've been slept in, and not just once. I'd hate to guess when you last washed your hair. You reek, Nat."

"Nice. Very encouraging. I don't pay you for style advice."

"And that's another thing. Lately, you don't pay me at all."

For once, the therapist's words broke through the thick wall she'd built between herself and the outside world. "What are you talking about?"

"Your last three checks have bounced." Kathy's voice softened, but it didn't lessen the humiliation.

Nat's cheeks burned. "Why didn't you say anything?"

"You haven't worked in over a year, and since you were self-employed, there's no disability insurance. I know things are tight, but I can't let this continue for much longer. My bookkeeper is already giving me grief."

"I'm sorry," she mumbled. "I had no idea."

"How about your other bills? Are they up to date?"

"I don't know." Nat turned away, studying one of Kathy's discount-house paintings. This one was a schooner or something. Some kind of ship, anyway. "I haven't exactly been opening my mail."

The therapist sighed. "Do you still have electricity? Heat? Water?"

"I think so. Like you pointed out, I haven't been bathing much."

"Will you at least *try* going back to work, even if it's part time? You need the money. And you need to dig yourself out of this rut."

Though her tendency was to pretend to consider Kathy's suggestions for a beat before nodding, Nat genuinely gave this one some thought, mostly because of the bounced checks. She recalled her life before Dyatlov: the thrill of an exciting scoop or impossible-to-get guest, the easy banter with Andrew, the constant offer of endorsements. It felt like that life belonged to someone else.

In many ways, it did. She wasn't that person anymore.

The idea of listening to other people's supernatural experiences, both real and imaginary, made her stomach churn. As the thought occurred to her, another image gained prominence—that of a creature dressed in human skin, with glowing yellow eyes....

Nat managed to grab her therapist's garbage can before she threw up.

* * *

Ordinarily she would have celebrated the small victory of a free ride home—Kathy had insisted on paying for a cab after the vomiting incident—but she was too miserable. The therapist had looked so guilty that Nat had been tempted to assure her the puke fest wasn't her fault, even though it was. If you hadn't been there; if you hadn't experienced the horror and witnessed your friends being slaughtered before your eyes, you couldn't possibly understand. Which was why she should give Igor a call. Out of all the people in this world, he was the only one who could understand what she was going through.

After she gave the driver her address, Nat pulled a flask from her purse and took a deep pull. *Just to rinse the taste from my mouth.* As she tucked it away, she caught the cabbie watching her in the rearview mirror. What was that expression? Sympathetic? Pitying? Judgmental? She hardly knew the difference anymore. But she was paying for this ride, goddammit (or Kathy was, and Lord knows she'd paid Kathy enough over the past year), and she deserved to enjoy it without some dude staring at her.

"Got a problem?" she snapped, and he took a breath as if to say something before shaking his head and returning his attention to the road. *Wise choice, buddy.*

She wondered what his reaction would be if she told him a murderer was behind him this very second. What if it wasn't a flask in her purse, but a knife? The flimsy plastic shield that separated them would hardly protect him. With a little force, a decent blade would go clear through it. What if she waited for an opportune moment—say, while crossing a busy intersection—before plunging the knife into his neck? That way, she could bring an end to them both.

Catching her line of thought, Nat forced herself to relax against the seat, reaching for her flask with shaking hands. What was wrong with her? All of a sudden, she was thinking like someone who needed more than a therapist. Like a padded room, for instance.

Besides, she wasn't a murderer. It had been a horrible accident, and she'd acted in self-defense. Her own lawyer had told her as much, and though he was paid to be on her side, he must have had a point since she'd gotten off with probation. Her victim's family had been outraged and heartbroken, but she wished she could have reassured them that she hadn't gotten off at all. She was a mess; just ask her therapist.

The cabbie pulled into her driveway at the same moment she drained the flask. Perfect timing.

"You live here?" he said, gazing at her with new respect. It made her hate him more. As your run-of-the-mill drunk, unwashed single woman, she wasn't worth the time of day, but now that she had a little money, she resembled a human being. What a twisted, fucked-up world they lived in.

"No, I plan on robbing the place and killing everyone inside." She closed the door harder than necessary, and as the driver peeled away, she could see him talking to someone. Probably the police. Like she cared—let them come. Perhaps they could help her move. The way Kathy had been talking, she couldn't afford to stay here much longer.

She'd paid off the house when things had been good, so she couldn't be evicted. The utilities could get shut off, like Kathy had intimated, or her insurance could run out, but that was about it. In a strange way, she wished for a mortgage, for a bank that would attach a glaring eviction notice to her door. Then she'd have an excuse to leave and never look back. But unless she took out a second mortgage and reneged on that, she was stuck with the place. God knows she didn't have the energy to move, not without a gun to her head.

Kicking aside the growing pile of flyers that blocked the front door, Nat pushed her way inside, locking the door behind her. A narrow path cut through the debris strewn over the staircase leading to her sanctuary. Grasping the railing, she hauled herself up, feeling like she was wearing concrete blocks instead of boots. Her heart pounded in rhythm with her aching head. She'd stopped buying the good stuff a while back, reasoning that it made no sense with the amount she was drinking. If she barely paused long enough to breathe, let alone taste, why waste the money? Besides, the more it burned, the more she liked it. It felt like punishment. She was self-flagellating her liver. The cheap crap was probably killing her, but she liked that too.

I can understand turning into a drunk, but must you be a slob too? Kathy's right. You do *reek. You used to have style, Nat. You were fierce—what happened to you?*

And that was the reason she wanted to leave this house as desperately as she'd once wanted to buy it. Andrew. Her friend was everywhere, his voice running constantly through her head, a never-ending stream of condemnation.

"Fuck off, Andy," she snarled, but under her sunglasses, her eyes filled with tears again. She wasn't fooling anyone, least of all herself. She'd give anything to have the real Andy back, even though he'd henpeck her to death. He would have forced her to get back to work by now, and if she could no longer handle the supernatural stuff, he would have come up with something else. That was his genius. He'd always told her he was the brains of the operation. Who knew he'd turn out to be right? Without him, she was nothing.

Stumbling to the sofa, she kicked off her wretched boots, wondering why she'd bothered to look presentable. She hadn't fooled anyone, including the cab driver.

"You're a born loser, kid," she said as she flopped facedown onto the couch she'd once paid thousands for, which was now stained with all manner of ick.

Would you please stop feeling sorry for yourself? Lots of people are worse off than you, princess. "Shut the fuck up, Andrew." She gave her friend's ghost the double bird before collapsing into drunken oblivion. That was why she drank, though she'd never be able to make Kathy or anyone else understand. Only by passing out did she have a hope in hell of shutting him up.

*   *   *

The phone woke her in the middle of the night.

Bleary-eyed, her head pounding worse than before, Nat groped for it, if just to stop the blaring. It felt like a fire engine was driving through her brain, sirens screeching.

Finally she found it, managing to hit the right button and hold it up to her ear. A win. "'Lo?"

"Is this Nat McPherson?" The woman's voice, clipped and formal, was enough to make her fury return. Why the hell was a telemarketer calling in the middle of the night? What was *wrong* with people?

"I'm not interested," she said and hung up, even though she heard the woman begging her to wait as she ended the call. The nerve of some people, seriously. It was enough to make her consider killing her phone plan. It wasn't like she wanted to talk to anyone anyway.

Before she could toss the cell across the room where it belonged, the sirens returned. Gritting her teeth until they made a scary cracking noise, Nat answered the call, planning to just as quickly end it.

"Please don't hang up! I need to talk to you." The woman's voice, tinny and disembodied, was audible, though Nat hadn't lifted the phone from her lap.

"I thought I told you I'm not interested."

"Please, you're the only one who can help me. June Garwin said I should call."

June Garwin. A blast from the past, a childhood friend. How long had it been since she'd spoken to June? Had to be over ten years. Why on earth would June tell anyone to call her?

"You'd better not be selling Tupperware."

"I'm not selling anything. I'm in trouble."

"Why are you calling me in the middle of the night? I haven't spoken to June in over a decade."

The caller hesitated before answering. "It's three o'clock in the afternoon. At least, it is here. What state are you in?"

Three in the afternoon? Then why was it so damn dark in here? She remembered the dirty sunglasses and tore them from her face, tossing them across the room and instantly regretting it. Sunlight was not her friend. Wincing, her head throbbing, she lay back on the couch.

"I still don't know why you're calling."

"My name is Riley. Riley Tanner. I could really use your help. I didn't know who else to call."

The woman's words brought to mind a different time, a different Nat. How often had she heard someone say the same thing, with that same air of desperation? *I didn't know who else to call. You're the only one who'll believe me. Everyone else thinks I'm crazy.*

She'd stopped caring about other people's problems some time ago, but she felt the slightest twinge of regret as she told this Riley Tanner, whoever she was, that she was wasting her time.

"Maybe the old Nat could have helped you," she said before she hung up, "but I'm not that person anymore."

CHAPTER TWO

She watched her husband pack for work with a heavy heart. How times had changed. She used to thrive during the days Jason was gone. Though she'd missed him, his absences gave her a chance to indulge in "Girls Only" movie nights with her daughter. Brooke, now ten, thought hanging out with Mom was a blast, but how much longer would that continue?

Riley had made it a habit to tackle household projects, read the thrillers she'd been looking forward to, and basically pamper herself until her husband returned. When other women asked her how she could stand being married to a long-haul trucker, she told them these mini "vacations" were the secret to a happy marriage. When it came to her and Jason, familiarity would never breed contempt—they simply weren't together enough. His homecoming was always treated as a special occasion, and she'd believed she had the best of both worlds: plenty of time to herself, and quality time with her husband when he came home.

But since they'd moved to the Oregon wilderness, his absences had become something to dread.

Jason dropped the stack of T-shirts he'd been holding with an exasperated sigh. "Okay, Ry, talk to me."

"What do you mean? I *have* been talking." Why did she bother playing dumb with Jason? It frustrated him more. He was too smart to fall for it, and besides, he knew her too well.

"You've been chattering. It's not the same thing. I want you to tell me what's bugging you, and don't tell me nothing, because you look like your best friend died."

"Don't even say that."

"What's going on? Is something wrong with Brooke?" He frowned, and she hated having to lay anything on him the night before he left. There was already enough on his mind, enough to keep track of.

"No, thank God. Brooke is great." *She really comes through for her mom when we're both screaming our heads off in terror.*

"What, then? Spit it out."

Riley shrugged, refusing to meet his eyes. No point helping him read her mind; he was adept enough at it. For the first time in years, she felt a flicker of resentment toward him. How come he got to leave while they had to stay here alone and deal with this? It wasn't fair. "There's no point talking about it."

"We have to talk about it, Riley—whatever *it* is. We talk about everything. You know that."

"Yeah, well, I've tried talking to you about this. It wasn't successful."

Moving his duffel bag aside, Jason sat beside her on the bed. "Try me again. I promise I'll listen."

She shook her head, clinging to her stubbornness, although she knew she wouldn't feel better until she'd told him what was on her mind. "I'm not in the mood to be ridiculed, thanks."

"Hey." Taking her chin in his hand, he gently turned her face toward him. "Who's ridiculing you? What are we talking about here?"

"You know…the fucking nightmare we go through whenever you leave."

He let go of her. "Is this about the animal again?"

The derision in his voice, whether real or imagined, was enough to make her blood boil. "It isn't an ordinary animal, Jason. I've *told* you that. See? This is why I didn't want to talk to you."

"Okay, okay." He lifted his hands in surrender. "Peace. I believe you, okay? You're not the type to imagine things that aren't there, and you've never been one to scare easily. I just don't understand why I've never seen it."

"Doesn't that prove there's something to it? If it were just an animal, it would show up when you're home. But it doesn't."

"So what do you want me to do? Do you want me to cancel the job?"

Her spirits soared at the thought of him staying with them for another week, but that would only delay the inevitable. Besides, they couldn't afford it. Though they'd gotten the world's best deal on the place (and now Riley was pretty sure she knew why), the mortgage payments stretched their budget to the breaking point. They desperately needed Jason's income. "I want you to believe me."

"I do believe you. I think there's probably a rational explanation, is all. Whatever it is, I'm sure it's not—"

"Stalking us. But that's exactly what it's doing. Plenty of animals stalk their prey, Jason. Trust me, whatever this thing is, it's malicious."

"If that's true, how can I leave?" Now it was his turn to avert his face, and she realized her husband had dismissed her concerns because that was the way he could travel hundreds of miles away from them.

"The same way we can stay. For now, at least, we have no choice."

* * *

"Mom?"

Riley made sure her tone was light, breezy, with no hint of the darkness that haunted her. Tonight's movie selection featured the latest teen sensations, but she couldn't have told you who a single one of them was. She'd absorbed about as much of the plot as she had Grade 12 algebra. "What's up, sweetie?"

"Are you okay?"

"Of course." Inside, a part of Riley flinched. She'd made it a point of pride never to lie to her daughter, a vow she'd rarely broken, and she was positive Brooke's older-than-her-years level of maturity was due in large part to this commitment. Children were much smarter and more capable than most people gave them credit for. "I miss your dad, but that's nothing new."

Partial truth is better than outright lie.

"Are you sure?" Her daughter chewed on a lock of her hair, a nasty habit Riley had thought she'd given up. Reaching over, she rescued the tendril, tucking it behind Brooke's ear.

"Why do you ask, hon?"

"Well…you don't normally bring a shotgun to Girls Only Night." She stared pointedly at the weapon Riley had leaned against an end table. "You're afraid it's going to come back, aren't you?"

"I don't know if it's going to come back or not." *Truth.* "But the gun is so we don't have to be afraid." *False. Gun or no gun, she was scared shitless.*

Whatever was stalking them wasn't your average forest critter. What if it wasn't an animal at all, but something monstrous, something that wasn't supposed to exist? If only Nat McPherson had agreed to help them, or at least hear her out. This wasn't the kind of thing you went running to a priest for. She needed an expert, and Nat was the closest thing she'd heard of.

"I'm scared," Brooke said, her voice quivering, and Riley gathered her daughter in her arms, riding a potent wave of rage and her own fear. She resisted the temptation to tell the girl she had nothing to be frightened of.

"I know, honey." She stroked her daughter's hair. "So am I."

"Did that Nat woman call back?"

Brooke had an uncanny ability to read her mind. Riley figured she must have inherited this trait from her dad. "No, not yet. But I'm not giving up."

After that first disastrous phone call, Nat had apparently put their number on her block list. Riley had left five messages, all of which had gone unreturned. At what point did she leave the realm of persistence and cross into stalking? The last thing they needed was for the McPherson woman to report them to the police, or worse yet, get a restraining order.

Thump.

A loud noise came from the front of the house, near the kitchen. Brooke froze, stiffening in her arms. "What was that?"

"Probably nothing. Could be the house settling, or a branch hitting the window. Pretty windy out there tonight."

Thump thump THUMP.

"If it's nothing, why do you have the gun?"

"Because my daddy didn't raise no fools." Flicking off the safety, Riley tucked the gun against her shoulder. Feeling silly, she crept toward the kitchen. "Stay here."

"The hell with that! I'm coming with you." Brooke hooked her finger into Riley's belt loop and crept along with her.

Though she wanted to protect her daughter from whatever was making the thumping noise, it was comforting to have her close. Reconciling herself to the fact that she was never going to be named Mother of the Year after this, she let Brooke accompany her.

They moved at an inebriated snail's pace, jumping whenever that ominous pounding started again. Riley flicked off the lights as she went, lessening the creature's advantage, but the darkness didn't make the situation any more reassuring.

"Mom? Do you think it can get in?" Brooke asked, her breath hot on Riley's neck.

"Don't worry about that. This house is solid as a rock." She hoped her daughter wouldn't notice that she'd answered without answering. Brooke had given voice to her own fears. What if that thing managed to make it inside? Would it attack them? Kill them? What did it want?

Brooke's fingers tightened on her belt loop as they entered the kitchen. A large bay window overlooked the sink, and Riley cursed herself for not closing the curtains. Even in the dark, whatever lurked outside would have full view of the room. She crouched, beginning to duck walk, and could tell by the adjusting pressure on her jeans that her daughter had done the same.

"Do you see anything?" she whispered, relying on her daughter's superior eyesight. Couldn't beat young eyes.

"No…do you?" She didn't sound as scared now, perhaps because the thumping noise appeared to have stopped. Maybe it *had* been the wind. Riley began to feel ridiculous. What was she doing, practically crawling on her own kitchen floor with a shotgun, and dragging her daughter along for the ride, as if they were playing soldier? Jason was right. If there was something out there, it was an animal—a bear, or maybe a puma. The big cats were rare in Oregon, but there had been sightings. It was possible. Certainly more possible than what she'd been thinking.

"I'm sorry, honey. This is silly. I'm afraid your mom overreacted." She began to straighten when Brooke's grip on her jeans tightened again, tugging downward. Her daughter made the strangest sound—like a scream but quiet, a frantic cry under her breath.

"T-the window." She gasped. "L-look."

Riley's attention snapped back to the window, and she stifled a cry of her own as she spotted the familiar, hideous silhouette. Something was out there, something that could see them perfectly, in spite of the darkness. As she stared at it, her heart pounding so hard it hurt, its gold eyes narrowed. An ordinary animal wasn't capable of looking that malicious. She hadn't been imagining it. Whatever was staring into her kitchen wasn't a bear or a puma. It had to be well over eight feet tall to be able to look into that window, for one thing.

"What *is* it?" Brooke hissed in her ear, and Riley wished she had an answer.

"I-I don't know."

As if it could hear them, the thing raised an oddly humanlike hand and slapped its palm against the window. *Thump.* They both flinched, close enough now to hear the scraping of its claws as it pulled away.

"W-what if it breaks it?"

Riley had been thinking the same. All this glass, the same glass that let in so much lovely light during the day, was their enemy once the sun set. It made them vulnerable. The creature had been hitting the window with some force. How long before a pane cracked?

Its eyes narrowed further as it leered at them. Once more, its hand rose, curling into a fist. *Thump.* And then, *thump-thump-THUMP*. She heard a creak as the pane protested, and her fear gave way to rage. How dare this ugly motherfucker threaten them in their own home? Who did it think it was?

What was *it?*

Fueled by anger, Riley leapt to her feet, ignoring her daughter's protests and tugs on her waistband. She brought the gun to her shoulder again. See how it managed to leer at them without a face.

"You are trespassing on private property," she yelled. Her voice was strong, fierce. "Go away now, or I'll shoot!" She leveled the shotgun at the thing's face, but rather than seem intimidated, it snarled, revealing a mouthful of very inhuman-like fangs. Its fingers tightened into a fist again, which it slammed against the window. *THUMP.* Riley heard the glass crack.

"Don't shoot, Mom! You'll break the window."

Brooke was right, of course. Before she could take a minute to think, to consider their situation, Riley reacted. Hot fury spiking through her veins, she rushed to the front door, oblivious to her daughter's pleas.

The night air was cool on her sweat-drenched skin. She swung the shotgun in the direction of the kitchen window, hands nerveless but steady. If she fired, she wouldn't miss. But there was nothing. Whatever had stood there seconds before was gone.

Riley retreated a step, making sure her back was against the house. The last thing she wanted was for it to get behind her. Eyes straining, she peered into the forest that surrounded them.

"Brooke, turn off the porch lights."

"Mom, *please* come back inside. Please!" Her daughter sounded like she was sobbing. Her terror stabbed at Riley, more painful than any physical malady, but she forced herself to ignore her child's cries. If she didn't take care of this now, whatever this thing was would continue to terrorize them whenever Jason was away. They couldn't go on like this. She would end it tonight or die trying.

"Do as I say, Brooke. *Now.*"

She could hear her daughter's whimpers, but the lights went out, plunging her into darkness. She hoped the creature wouldn't attack before her eyes had a chance to adjust.

What was that?

A sly rustling sound to her left. An intake of breath. Riley swung the gun in that direction and fired.

* * *

This time it *was* the middle of the night when her phone rang, or nearly. Nat squinted at the call display, her temper rising. Some people couldn't take a damn hint, but that was okay. She was through ignoring it. This chick was going to get a piece of her mind, and it was not going to be a pretty one.

She gripped the phone so hard she heard the plastic crack. "Listen, Mrs—"

But this wasn't the woman. It was a child. Screaming.

"Please help me. There's a creature outside and it's killing my mom! You have to help us, please."

Nat straightened, instantly sober. "Where are you?"

"I'm in the house, but my mom went outside with the gun and I heard her shoot." The girl wailed. "Please help us."

Jesus Christ. Why were people so damn stupid? Why hadn't Tanner stayed in the house? Still, part of her could understand. Sometimes you got tired of being scared. She hoped the woman's foolishness hadn't turned this weeping girl into an orphan. "Can you see your mom? Don't leave the house—look out a window. Can you see anything?"

"S-she made me turn off the lights." The girl sobbed, and Nat could hear her struggling for breath. "E-everything's dark. I haven't heard anything since the gun went off."

Fuck. This wasn't good. This wasn't good at all. The gun had probably been plucked from her mother's hands and used against her. Leaning forward, Nat resolved herself. It was too late for the mother, but maybe she could save this girl. "What's your name?"

"B-Brooke."

"Okay, Brooke. I need you to do something for me, okay? I need you to lock the door. Keep the lights off."

"B-but my mom's out there." Her voice rose into a wail again. "I-I can't leave her out there."

"She'll knock when she's ready to come in," Nat said, crossing her fingers. "You'll know it's her, because the creature won't knock." *I hope.* "But you need to lock the door."

"I-I can't. I'm scared."

"I know you are, sweetie, but you have to. Do it for your mom. Your mom wouldn't want anything to happen to you." She pictured the girl on the other end of the phone. She sounded so young. Nat hoped her mom was alive, but at this point, the prospects didn't seem good. "Go on, I'll wait."

After what felt like an interminably long time, the girl returned. "Okay, I locked the door."

"Good. Now I need you to hang up and call 9-1-1, okay?"

"They won't come." Her voice broke again, and Nat wondered how much more the girl could handle. She was a child. Children shouldn't have to be this scared or this brave, ever. "We're too far out of town. By the time they get here, it'll be too late."

"Call them anyway, okay? Maybe they're closer than you think, but you won't know until you try. *Call* them."

"But—you'll help us, won't you? You have to help my mom."

Nat winced. If only she'd listened to what the woman had been telling her. If only she'd done the right thing. Now it was too late to help Riley Tanner.

But it wasn't too late for her daughter.

"Call 9-1-1, sweetie. Please."

"Promise you'll help us. Promise you'll come." The girl was in hysterics now, barely understandable.

"If I promise, will you call them?"

"Y-yes."

So Nat promised, right before her phone went dead.

God help us all.

CHAPTER THREE

The woman threw her arms around her, pulling her into a bear hug so tight it squeezed her breath from her. Nat, never a demonstrative person at the best of times, reluctantly allowed herself to be hugged. After all, how often did someone return from the dead?

Though it meant she'd been held to her promise, she was damn grateful Riley Tanner was alive.

"Thank you so much for coming. You don't know how much this means to us."

"Thank your daughter. It was her doing."

"Sorry about that. You were the last person I called, and she hit redial in her panic…"

"I think she knew *exactly* what she was doing."

The girl in question hung back, smiling shyly. She was taller than Nat had expected, and older. Pretty, with long brown hair pulled into a ponytail. She looked innocent, how kids used to look before they all started dressing like twenty-year-olds. This one didn't look to be in a hurry to grow up, and Nat was glad for it. Being an adult was no picnic. She'd never understood why most kids were in such a rush to join the ranks.

"You must be Brooke."

"Hi." The girl lowered her eyes. "Thanks for coming."

"You're welcome. I'm just relieved you're both okay."

The last thing she needed was another death on her conscience.

"We're alive, thank God, but barely. I never want to be that scared again." Riley ran a hand through her hair with a rueful smile.

"Me neither. I thought my heart was going to stop," Brooke said, temporarily forgetting her shyness.

"It only feels that way." Nat knew from experience how much the human heart could take and keep on going. Maybe the very ill or elderly could be scared to death, but a girl this young and healthy? It would take a lot more than fear.

"Do you have any other bags?" Riley asked, glancing at Nat's backpack.

"Just one. It's small. I-I wasn't sure how long I'd be staying."

"Oh, don't worry about that." Riley touched her arm. "We have plenty of room."

The woman's warmth was genuine, and it was beginning to thaw the wall of ice around Nat, in spite of her resistance. Maybe it would be good for her to get away, exactly what Kathy had been saying all along. She hadn't touched a drop of alcohol since Brooke phoned, and had managed to pay a few bills and wash her hair. Her therapist would be proud.

She'd been afraid she wouldn't be able to stop drinking on her own, but it had been easier than she'd thought. She'd never made a great alcoholic. Once this was over, she'd have to find a better way to kill herself.

"What were you thinking, going after that thing with a gun?" No matter how nice the woman was, Nat had to make sure she understood how serious this was. She couldn't bear to see another person killed. "You're lucky to be alive." She averted her attention from the woman to the baggage carousel, struggling to keep her anger in check.

"I know; I know." Riley gathered her daughter close in a one-armed hug. "I've been told."

"I need to make sure we're on the same page. I don't want you going after it like that again. Don't you realize how strong these things are? If it had decided to take that gun from you, you wouldn't have stood a chance." *Ah, at last.* There was her damn bag. She pushed forward to snag her suitcase, ignoring the dirty looks she got from the sheeple clustered around the carousel.

"Got it," Nat said, and then noticed both Brooke and Riley were gawking at her like she'd grown a second head. "What?"

Brooke was the first to speak. "You said 'these things.' You know what they are?"

She sighed. *Here we go.* "Based on what you've both described, and where we're located, I'd say we're dealing with a Sasquatch." Though she'd lowered her voice, she expected the other passengers to be giving her that second-head look too, but no one paid them any attention.

"I *told* you," Brooke said, poking her mother's arm. "That's what *I* thought it was. At least someone believes us now. Even Dad won't listen to us."

Nat raised an eyebrow at Riley. "Your husband hasn't seen it?"

She shook her head. "That's part of the problem. It bothers us when Jason is out of town, but unfortunately, he's out of town a lot."

"Dad's a long-haul trucker," Brooke added, an obvious note of pride in her voice.

Nat frowned. If the creature knew when the man of the house was absent, it was watching them. *Stalking* them, just as Riley had said. That wasn't good. She was hardly an expert, but everything she'd heard or read about the Sasquatch indicated they were shy creatures, more afraid of humans than humans were of them. Why was this one behaving so aggressively? What had attracted it to the house?

"I definitely believe you, but that might be all I'm able to offer. I was a podcaster, not a cryptozoologist, and I'm not even a podcaster anymore."

"You'll be able to help us," Brooke said. "I just know it."

Riley didn't look as certain as her daughter, but that was a good thing. Nat didn't want these women thinking she was a superhero. She'd quickly disappoint them.

"Come on, let's get out of here," Riley said. "I can't wait to show you the house."

* * *

Riley's husband Jason seemed nice enough. He couldn't help being an idiot.

That's how Nat had come to think of people like him, morons who refused to believe in anything unless it was standing right in front of them. She didn't get it. How could you love someone enough to marry them, but not enough to believe them? Jason presumably knew Riley wasn't insane, and that she wasn't given to hallucinations. And what about his daughter? If he mistrusted his wife, for whatever reason, why wouldn't he believe Brooke? Why was it always dudes who were the unbelievers? Why didn't men believe women? It drove her crazy.

"So you're the monster hunter," he'd said when they were introduced, giving her a lazy grin he likely thought was charming. But she was in no mood to be charmed.

"First of all, I'm not a hunter. Second of all, this isn't a monster. And third, I'd like to see how long you'd remain skeptical if one of these things was ripping your best friend's guts out."

Jason's mouth fell open, and that dumb grin vanished from his face, just as she'd hoped. His daughter snickered, elbowing him in the ribs. "She told *you*, Dad."

Their relationship hadn't had the most auspicious beginning. But she'd like to think he'd warm up to her.

"Would you like a drink, Ms. McPherson?" he asked when she came downstairs after her shower.

"Water is fine, thanks." No sense tempting fate. "And you can call me Nat."

"I hope you don't mind if I have one. I have a feeling I'm going to need it."

She shrugged, though watching him drink was going to be torture. "Go ahead, it's your house. Knock yourself out."

"Please, sit down." Riley gestured to the overstuffed sofa. "Make yourself at home. Are you hungry?"

Nat couldn't remember the last time she'd had a decent meal, or had felt like eating, but as if Riley's words were magic, her stomach rumbled. "A little bit, maybe, but I'm fine with the water for now."

Jason handed her a tumbler full of ice water as Riley put a dish of mixed nuts in front of her. "Please help yourself. We're pretty informal around here," she said.

Grabbing a handful of nuts, Nat leaned back on the couch and surveyed the room as she munched. It was a beautiful home, all that gleaming blond wood and huge windows. Sadly, the windows were a liability. They turned the house into a fishbowl. She could understand why Riley had fallen in love with the place, though. If she hadn't been such a city girl, she might have been tempted herself.

Once the Tanners had drinks and had seated themselves around her, she decided it was time to learn what she was dealing with. She turned to Riley. "You said on the phone that you think the real estate agent tricked you. What exactly did he tell you about the history of this place?"

"Not much, and not for lack of trying. I knew the price was too low, knew it was too good to be true, but he kept insisting there wasn't a catch. Finally, he admitted that the previous owners left because the woman was frightened by what he called 'night noises.'" She hooked her fingers in the air, putting quotes around *night noises*. "He claimed she was some soft city person, scared off by the local wildlife. But he wouldn't tell me what the local wildlife was."

"Well, this is wildlife, all right." Nat felt her temper return. The real estate agent had found a sucker, and he'd known it. Question was, had he believed the wildlife story? Or was he aware of what they were dealing with? Any information would be helpful, as long as it wasn't a bunch of bullshit. "Do you think we could arrange a meeting with this real estate agent? I'd like to talk to him."

"I don't think he'll be much help to you," Jason said. "Once the girls started having problems, I went back to the guy, tried to see if there was any way we could get out of the deal, or at least get some of our money back."

"I take it he wasn't cooperative."

He grimaced. "That's an understatement. And now we're stuck with the place, unless we can find other buyers who aren't from around here."

"I don't want to let this...*thing* chase us away from our home. It's *our* home." Nat recognized the set of Riley's jaw. This woman was every bit as stubborn as she was. Her persistence with the phone calls should've tipped her off.

"That's partly what bothers me. If this has been going on for some time, before you were here, this creature has attached itself to the house for whatever reason. It's not normal behavior. If it *is* a Sasquatch, they normally do everything they can to avoid human contact, but this one appears to be seeking you out."

Nat had expected Jason to laugh when she'd said *Sasquatch*, or at least smirk, but perhaps he was smarter than she'd given him credit for, because he did neither.

"Why haven't I seen it?" he asked. "I've stayed up nights, watching for it, but it only shows up when I'm gone."

"That worries me too," she admitted. "The fact that it reveals itself when you're not here means it's watching your family pretty closely." She didn't miss Brooke's shudder. "Are you sure you want to be here for this?"

The girl nodded. "Nothing could be scarier than what happened last week."

Nat hoped she was right, but she had her doubts. "Unless…do you have a regular schedule for when you go out of town?"

"Nah, I wish." Jason took a long pull from his beer. "I go when they call me. Usually it's a few times a month, but I never know until they call."

"Then it's watching the house. And it's obviously decided you're the biggest threat, which means it can tell the difference between male and female."

"But that's impossible, isn't it?" Riley asked. "Can animals do that?"

"Sure. There are baboons in Africa who will attack groups of women but leave a single man alone. Animals aren't stupid, but for some reason, it makes us feel better to believe they are," Nat said. "Also, since no one has had the opportunity to study these creatures, there's no way of knowing how intelligent they are, or what they're capable of. If you think about it, the fact they've gone this long without their existence being officially confirmed proves their intelligence."

"Or brings their existence into question." Jason drained his beer, setting the bottle on the coffee table.

"Well, what do *you* think it is? I'd love to hear your theory." She hoped he wouldn't say that both his wife and daughter were imagining things. It would be a shame to have to kill him.

"Damned if I know." He shrugged, looking uncomfortable. "I admit I thought it was a bear at first. Maybe a puma, or even coyotes. But the damn thing is tall enough to look in our kitchen window, so now I don't know what it is."

"Back when I used to host my podcast, I'd get tons of calls from people in Oregon who claimed they'd seen a Sasquatch," Nat said. "Sightings in this area are some of the highest in the world. Did either of you get a good look at it?" She returned her focus to Brooke and Riley.

The girl shook her head. "It had yellow eyes. That's all I saw. They glowed."

The words jolted Nat like an electric current. *Yellow eyes...they glowed.* The first time she'd seen glowing yellow eyes, people had died. *Andrew* had died.

"Are you all right?" Riley touched her arm, hesitantly, as if afraid Nat might bite. "You look like you've seen a ghost."

She forced herself to snap out of it. That was then, and this was now. She wasn't in Russia, and this wasn't the Dyatlov Pass. Whatever creature was terrorizing the Tanners, it wasn't the same. Couldn't be.

"I'm fine, thanks. Just a little PTSD."

"What happened to you?" Brooke asked.

"Brooke..." her mother warned.

"No, it's okay." Nat made herself smile, hoping it appeared somewhat natural. "Creatures with glowing yellow eyes killed my best friend, along with a few other people. It happened right in front of me. But don't worry," she hastened to add, seeing the horrified expressions on the family's faces, "I'm positive this creature is something else."

"But what if it's not?" If Brooke's eyes got any larger, they'd swallow the poor kid's face. "What if it's the same?"

"It's not," Nat said.

"But how do you *know* it's not the same?"

"Because I killed it."

This was followed by a long, awkward silence. Finally, Jason spoke.

"So I was right. You *are* a monster hunter." He winked at her.

Nat let herself relax. These were good people. They weren't going to doubt her story, or assume she was crazy. They weren't going to call her a liar. They'd asked for her help. They respected her experience, her knowledge. "Not by choice."

"There was something else. It was the way it looked at us—I don't quite know how to explain it without sounding insane, but—it looked like it hated us," Riley said, taking a hurried sip of her mixed drink. "It narrowed its eyes at me like it wanted to rip my head off."

Brooke nodded. "Totally. It was evil. You could tell." She shuddered again, and glanced at her mom's drink, probably wishing she was old enough to knock a few back.

Don't start, kid. It's a dead end.

Despite her resistance to revisiting the past, Nat couldn't help thinking back to Dyatlov. Those creatures had been killing machines, but that was just it—there had been something robotic about the carnage. It hadn't felt personal, or malicious. They'd been dumb animals, acting on instinct. What Riley and Brooke were describing was much more unsettling.

"Anything else? How big was it?" she asked, trying her best to keep the concern out of her voice.

"It had to be at least eight feet tall, since its head reached the top of the kitchen window. And its head was quite round, rounder than a human head would be," Riley said. "It was big too." She held her hands apart to indicate the size. "About as big as a watermelon."

Ugh. Why did these guys always have to be huge? "Any facial characteristics? Was it covered in hair?"

"I couldn't see. It was always too dark." She looked over at her daughter, but Brooke shook her head.

"Wait a second," the girl said, brightening. "I saw its hands. They had fingers, just like a person's."

"That's right. They were dark and leathery, with long claws at the ends. Before I ran outside, the thing made a fist and pounded on the window," Riley said.

"Damn thing cracked the pane. When you find it, tell it that it owes me a new window," Jason joked, but no one laughed.

Especially not Nat, who was remembering other clawed hands, hands that could remove a man's head with one swipe.

"Did you find any prints?" she asked.

"Once. They were underneath all the windows, as if it had used different ones to watch us throughout the night," Riley said, growing pale. It was clear how frightened she was, and Nat wondered again how Jason could have doubted her. Whatever was scaring the women in this house was very real.

"But we always get so much rain up here. By the time Jason got home, they were long gone."

"How big were they?"

Again, Riley used her hands to indicate the size. "Huge."

"Did they look like paws, or…"

"Like feet. Bare feet. With a long claw on the big toe."

"From what you're telling me, it certainly sounds like a Sasquatch, or some kind of large apelike creature. Whether you call it Sasquatch, Yeti, or Bigfoot, the descriptions are all pretty much the same," Nat said. "Apes have hands and fingers and toes like our own, so the prospect of another creature having them is not that strange. No claws, though." The next she said for Jason's benefit. "What we think of as 'monsters' are creatures that haven't been officially categorized yet, and scientists are the first to admit that new species are being discovered all the time. To assume we've found everything there is to find is arrogant at best, and stupid at worst."

"Okay, saying I accept there is such a creature around here—*something* cracked that window, and it wasn't Riley or Brooke—what does it want?" Jason asked. "How can we make it go away and leave us alone?"

Three pairs of eyes focused on her, waiting for her to tell them what they needed to know, to give them hope. Unfortunately for the Tanners, Nat was more like Riley than any of them knew. She didn't like to lie to people either.

"Those are great questions," she said. "I wish I had the answers for you."

CHAPTER FOUR

Her foot was on fire.

She shrieked in agony. The pain was excruciating. Frantically, she fought to free herself, trying to kick, but she was trapped, pinned. The flames climbed up her leg. She could smell the stench of her own flesh as it burned.

But wait—this wasn't how it was supposed to happen. Steven was supposed to rescue her from the tent. *Where was he?*

As the last of her boot burned away, the fire began to devour her bare flesh. Indescribable pain. Unable to escape, she could do nothing but lie in the snow and wait to die. And scream.

Warm yellow light blinded her. Had the fire reached her face so quickly? She covered her head with her arms, fighting to survive though it was pointless. She was already dead. She'd died on Dyatlov Pass.

"Nat! Nat, wake up." Someone shook her, but gently. *Steven?* The pain receded. Her foot ached, but the sharp edge of the agony had dulled. She slowly lowered her arms, squinting at a woman she didn't quite recognize. Then she focused enough to see the long, dark hair. *Anubha?* Had the Inuit tracker survived after all?

More faces appeared behind the woman. A man, and a girl. Who was the girl? There hadn't been a child on their expedition.

Then Nat remembered where she was. Her face burning in a different way, she sat up. "Night terrors," she mumbled. "It's part of the PTSD. I'm sorry to have woken you."

"Don't worry about it. Are you all right? You're burning up." Riley pressed her hand to Nat's forehead, an oddly motherly gesture from a woman who was probably the same age.

"I was dreaming my foot was on fire—that's probably why." She tried to laugh it off, but didn't quite make it. Her breathing was too ragged.

"Oh my God. That's horrible." Riley made a face. "Is that what happened to you?"

So she'd noticed the limp. "No. I mean, it could have happened, but one of the guys in my group pulled me out of danger before it did. I lost a couple of toes from frostbite, though. They hurt sometimes, and I forget they're not there." Seeing the anxious faces surrounding her, she attempted a grin. "Sorry to have scared you, but I warned you, I'm not the best houseguest."

"You are too the absolute bestest houseguest!"

"Listen to Brooke," Jason said, resting his hands on his daughter's shoulders. "She's the smart one in the family. Do you want that drink now? No offence, but you look like you could use one."

The way her mouth watered at the thought was scarier than the foot-on-fire nightmare. "Thanks, but no thanks. As much as I'd love one, I was starting to get into trouble with that, so I stopped."

Jason colored. "I'm sorry; I didn't realize."

"Don't apologize, please. It was probably an overreaction on my part, but I have enough problems, as you're starting to see." Running a hand through her hair, she hated how awkward this was. This was exactly why she loathed leaving her comfort zone. Why couldn't she be normal again? Well, not that she'd ever been *normal*-normal. She was a woman in her mid-thirties, never married, with no kids, who'd made her living discussing the supernatural online. Her constant companion had been a twenty-four-year-old gay man who'd driven her crazy more days than not.

And she'd give everything to return to those days.

The old Nat, she had been a fun kind of weird. People had thought of her as *quirky* or *eccentric*, not *damaged*.

Or dangerous.

In spite of the compassion the Tanners had shown her, she could see it on their faces. The fear, the doubt. Had they done the right thing, welcoming her into their home? Or was the creature within worse than the one outside? Could Brooke be safe with this insane chick sleeping in the next room?

"I understand if you're no longer comfortable with me staying here. I can leave in the morning."

"What are you talking about?" Riley asked, appearing genuinely surprised. "You had a nightmare. We've all had them. It's not a big deal."

"Yes, you're not getting rid of us that easy," Jason said. "You're stuck with us."

"I think it's the other way around." Night terrors weren't the same as ordinary nightmares. She was fairly certain no one in the Tanner family had woken up screaming, positive they were on fire. "Are you sure?"

Riley squeezed her hand. "Of course we're sure."

"Here." Brooke held out a creature of a different sort, a purple hippo whose large mouth curved upward in a smile. Nat reached for it, her fingers sinking into the soft plush.

"That's nice of you, Brooke, but I'm sure Ms. McPherson doesn't want your doll."

"Tulip is not a *doll*," Brooke said, rolling her eyes at her father. "She's a *hippo*, obviously. And she's super brave. She chases nightmares away."

"Really?" Nat studied the hippo in her hands with new respect. "That *is* brave. I'd be honored to share my bed with her, thank you. And please, call me Nat."

Brooke shot her father a triumphant look that clearly said, *"See?"*

"Are you sure we can't get you anything else? Some water? Maybe it's too dark in here—would a nightlight help?" Riley asked, her face set in worried lines.

Touched, Nat patted her hand. "I'm fine, really. I'm just sorry to have woken you."

"We don't sleep well anyway," Brooke said. "Not since…well, you know."

"Nat's not going to sleep well, either, if we keep bothering her. Let's give her some space." Riley touched the top of her head, once again making Nat feel like she was a pampered child instead of an unwanted, damaged adult. "Goodnight. If you need anything, just holler."

"Will do. Goodnight."

When the lights were off again and the door had shut behind the Tanners, leaving her alone, Nat breathed a sigh of relief, settling back onto the pillows. She had to be careful. It would be too easy to forget she was here because of something horrifying. In spite of what they'd experienced, this family was so grounded, so enviably normal. And with Jason at home, the creature would be keeping its ugly head down for a while.

Nat turned on her side and closed her eyes, snuggling close to the stuffed hippo.

Brooke had been right about Tulip.

For once, there were no more nightmares.

* * *

Nat could tell right away that something was wrong. Riley wasn't a woman who hid her emotions. Her distress was written all over her face.

"What is it?" she asked, keeping her voice low since Jason was on the phone. She'd slept longer than she'd intended, better than she had in over a year. She'd have to tell Brooke how effective her hippo had been, but she had a feeling the girl already knew. "What's wrong?"

They've talked it over and decided you're right; it's too much of a risk having you here. They want you to leave.

"It's Dad's work," Brooke whispered. "He's getting called on another job."

Nat felt chilled fingers creep along her spine. "So soon?"

"It's always so unpredictable," Riley said. "We can never count on how long he'll be home. They can call for him at any time."

Jason ended his call and joined them at the kitchen table. "Sorry, guys, but I'm afraid the party's over." Seeing Nat, he nodded in her direction. "Morning. Like some coffee?"

"That would be great, thanks." As well as she'd slept, she was groggy. Caffeine would clear the cobwebs from her brain.

"When do you have to leave?" Riley asked.

"Crack of dawn tomorrow. Sorry, babe, but we need the money. The mortgage payment is coming up, and we're short. How do you take it, Nat?"

"Black, please." Riley looked so upset that she wasn't sure it was the best time to speak up, but she had to chance it. "Don't worry; we're going to be fine." She wrapped her hands around the steaming cup Jason gave her, feeling better before taking a sip. Such was the power of coffee. "Thank you."

"Are you sure?" Riley asked her. "The last time that thing paid us a visit, I shoved a gun in its face. It's bound to be pissed off. More than it already was."

"Of course I'm sure. This is why you brought me here, remember? The family bonding has been fun, but I can't help you if I don't at least get a look at this thing, and as long as Jason's here, it'll stay in hiding."

The man in question frowned. "I don't like the idea of leaving the three of you here to deal with this on your own."

Nat bit her lip. Jason's long absences were clearly a source of conflict in the family, and it wasn't her place to say anything. Then again, she'd never been one to keep her mouth shut. "But don't you always leave them to deal with this on their own? How is this time any different, except for the fact I'm here?"

She'd expected an angry response, but Jason just looked miserable. Miserable and guilty. "It's different now. That thing nearly broke the window trying to get in last time. My wife started carrying her gun around. My daughter is scared to death." He ran his hands through his wavy dark hair, pulling at it. "What am I supposed to do? I *have* to work."

Riley rested her hand on her husband's arm. "We understand, Jay. We know you'd stay here with us if you could. This was no one's choice."

"If it makes you feel any better, I don't think it was trying to get in," Nat said.

All three Tanners stared at her.

"It pounded on the window until it cracked," Jason said.

"I realize that, but consider how strong this creature is." Nat refused to call it a *thing*. It was a living, breathing entity, even if they weren't sure what it was. "If it really wanted to get in, it would have. It wouldn't have settled for banging on the kitchen window."

"What does it want, then? Why won't it leave us alone?" Riley's voice broke, and for the first time, Nat saw the fear behind the woman's bravery.

"That's what I'm hoping to find out. A lot of creatures are territorial. Maybe it feels this is its territory, and it's trying to scare you off. Or maybe it's curious, and pounded on the window when it felt threatened. It didn't approach you when you went outside, did it?"

"No. The only creature I encountered was a snuffling raccoon. A raccoon that's damn lucky I was a lousy shot that night." Riley attempted a smile, but her lips trembled. Nat's arrival obviously hadn't helped her feel more confident about facing the creature. She tried not to take it personally.

"But you're not going to do something that reckless again, right?" Nat had to be sure she didn't need to worry about Riley going renegade on top of everything else.

She was shocked when Riley hesitated—not that the woman would put herself at risk again (she knew a stubborn woman when she saw one), but that she'd actually admit it.

"Riley?" Jason pressed.

Meeting his eyes, the woman lifted her chin. "I'll do what I have to in order to protect my family."

Jason looked like she had slapped him across the face. "*Your* family? It's yours now? What about me?"

"Of course it's yours too, but you're not going to be here."

"That's not fair, Riley. One of us has to work."

She glared at him. "That's not fair, either. I can't help it that business has been slow. No one has the money to hire outside design help anymore."

"Then maybe you need a different career."

"Will you guys *stop*?" Brooke cried out, pushing back from the table. "I hate it when you fight."

It wasn't Nat's favorite thing, either. She was sorry she'd put Riley on the spot in front of Jason, but she wouldn't make that mistake again.

Her daughter's distress deflated Riley, who took hold of Brooke's arm before she could leave. "Sorry, honey. Everyone's a bit on edge. Please stay. Why don't I make some pancakes? I have some wild blueberries in the fridge."

Wild blueberry pancakes sounded amazing to Nat, whose appetite had returned with a vengeance. But sadly, Jason wasn't biting.

"Promise me you won't go after it on your own again. I couldn't stand it if something happened to you."

"You don't understand what it's been like. *Neither* of you do." Riley narrowed her eyes at Jason and Nat, making it clear her guest was on the shit list too. "You weren't here. You don't know what it's like to feel like a victim in your own home, night after night. Well, I got tired of it. Sue me."

For a moment, Nat was unable to speak. *She* didn't know what it felt like? Was this woman serious?

"*I* was here, Mom. You said we'd stick together, and then you ran off and left me by myself." Tears spilled over Brooke's lashes and trickled down her cheeks. "I didn't know if you were alive or dead. How do you think that made me feel?"

"I'm sorry, honey. You're right; that wasn't fair. I wanted to put an end to this." She sighed, burying her face in her hands. "I'm so tired of being afraid."

"Trust me—you don't want to make an enemy if you don't have to. Other than the last time, when it cracked the window, had it ever shown aggression before?" Nat asked.

Brooke glanced at her mother before responding. "N-no. It just looked at us."

"Did it pound on the window before you pointed the gun at it, or after?"

Riley hesitated. "I'm not sure."

"Mom, you pointed the gun at it first, remember? When we went into the kitchen to see what was making the thumping noise, you had the gun with you."

Ah, from the mouths of babes. Well done, Brooke. Nat had guessed the answer, but she also could tell Riley didn't want to admit it. It was better to blame this whole situation on the nasty creature.

"But doesn't the thumping noise prove it was pounding on the window before it saw us?" Riley crossed her arms, clearly not willing to give up without a fight. "That it was being aggressive before it saw the gun?"

"It *was* really loud," Brooke said. "It shook the whole house."

"Not necessarily. Assuming this creature isn't aware of its own strength, which is likely, that could have been its way of getting your attention."

Riley snorted. "It got our attention, all right."

"I realize how frightening it must have been to have it peering at you through the window—I *do* understand," Nat said. "But it sounds like it's curious. Maybe it's bored. It acted with aggression when it felt under threat. I'm guessing it's seen guns before."

"How do you know for sure?" Jason asked.

"I don't. Not really. It's an educated guess, and I won't be able to do better until I see it for myself. But I'd suggest not threatening it. I think there's a good chance you could live in harmony with this creature, as strange as it sounds." Nat surveyed the Tanners, hoping her words were having some impact, but only Brooke appeared receptive.

"What if you're wrong? What if it wants to hurt us, or it's territorial, like you said, and it wants to scare us off?" Riley said.

Nat shrugged. "Then we'll have to kill it."

CHAPTER FIVE

When Jason left, a shadow fell over the house. After the argument at the breakfast table, the family never recaptured the lighthearted friendliness Nat had thought was their norm. There was tension between Riley and Jason, tension between Brooke and Riley, and as much as she didn't want to admit it, tension between herself and Riley. She could feel resentment radiating off the woman in waves, but told herself to ignore it. She'd been hired to do a job, and that's what she needed to focus on. It wasn't necessary for her and Riley to be friends, or even get along. Perhaps it was best if she maintained her distance.

At least Brooke was talking to her.

"What's that?" the girl asked, staring at the contraption in Nat's arms. She hovered outside the guestroom, as if she wanted to come in but wasn't sure she was welcome.

"This? It's an infrared, motion-sensitive camera. I'm going to rig it up outside the kitchen window, see if I can get some pictures of our Bigfoot."

"Cool! Do you think it'll work?" Brooke craned her neck for a better look, and Nat waved her inside, handing her the valuable piece of equipment.

"It should. The photographs won't be the best. They'll be grainy, and since it's infrared, they'll look pretty weird, but it's better than nothing. This camera has a no-glow or invisible flash, because we don't want a regular flash going off, alerting the creature that we're taking pictures of it."

"Will that make it mad?" Spotting her purple hippo on Nat's bed, Brooke seized it and cuddled it close.

"It might, but I'm more worried about the creature destroying the camera—and the photographs. There's a reason no one's gotten a great photo of these guys. Let's just say they *really* don't like having their picture taken."

Satisfied her camera and other gear was in order, Nat pulled on a jacket. Though it was late summer, the house was so sheltered that the temperatures dipped drastically in the afternoon. "Want to help? I could use a hand."

Brooke brightened, appearing happier than she had since the argument. "Sure."

In spite of the tension in the house, Nat felt better than she had in months. Not drinking might have had a lot to do with it, but there was something about human companionship too. She realized again exactly how much she'd lost when Andrew died. He'd not only been her business partner and friend, but also her main social contact. It wasn't good for her to be so isolated. Once she got home, she'd have to change that.

She couldn't imagine replacing him, even in title. The idea of hiring another producer was abhorrent. But maybe an assistant? Nat caught herself considering going back to work and had to stifle a laugh so Brooke wouldn't think she was crazy.

"What's so funny?" Brooke asked.

"Nothing, really. I guess I'm finding it pretty amazing how much better I've been feeling since I got here." After lacing up her hiking boots, Nat led the way outside and headed to the kitchen window. Thankfully, luck was with her. An ancient oak tree stood nearby, its trunk too wide for Nat to get her arms around. The perfect place to hide her camera.

"That's a good thing, isn't it?" Brooke's forehead wrinkled in confusion.

"Yes, it's a good thing. It's a bit surprising, is all."

"Why weren't you feeling good before?"

Nat hesitated, wondering how much she should say. She wasn't going to rehash the whole gory story, not to anyone, and certainly not to a child. "I lost my best friend last year. I've had a hard time getting over it."

"I'm sorry. Did...did she die?"

"Yes, he did. He was more than my best friend, though. He was my business partner too." She laughed, trying to diffuse the somber mood. "Hell, I don't know why I keep calling him my *best* friend. Turns out he was my only friend."

"That's not true." Brooke took Nat's hand, giving it a gentle squeeze. "I'm your friend."

"Thanks, Brooke. That means a lot to me." She turned away, feeling a burning sensation in her eyes. "Let's get this camera mounted before it gets dark, okay?"

"Okay." Brooke nodded, giving Nat's hand another squeeze before she let go.

Taking a deep breath, Nat searched for handholds in the bark, wishing she'd thought to bring a pair of gloves. The tree's surface was rough. It was going to do a number on her skin. Grabbing one of the lower branches, she hoisted herself up. It had been forever since she'd climbed a tree, but she'd hoped it was one of those riding-a-bicycle things you never forgot, and so far, it appeared to be. When she estimated she was about fifteen feet off the ground, she searched for a good, sturdy branch to hook the camera to. It had to be concealed from view but have a clear shot of the kitchen window. No point taking a bunch of photos of foliage.

Seeing one a few feet above her, she steeled herself and continued to climb. Brooke picked up on her trepidation. "Be careful!"

The worst part wasn't the climbing. It was stretching herself along the limb so she could hang the camera near the end of the branch. She tested it, pressing down on it with increasing strength, but couldn't move it. When she'd convinced herself it was stable, she wiped the sweat out of her eyes and gripped it with her hands and feet, beginning to inch along it.

"You're scaring me," Brooke cried. Her voice sounded like it was coming from far below—*too* far. Nat told herself not to look down.

"Almost done," she called back, fighting to keep her voice from wavering.

As she steadied the camera, a loud noise startled her, and she fumbled, grasping the branch with both hands to keep from falling. The camera started to fall and she swiped for it, managing to catch it by the strap while Brooke shrieked below her.

"I'm okay; I'm okay." Nat rested her cheek against the branch for a moment, willing her heart to slow down. It felt like it was about to explode out of her chest. "What the hell was that?"

"I-I don't know." Poor kid sounded terrified. "Will you come down now, please?"

"One more sec. I have to attach the camera." Though she'd like nothing more than to plant her feet back on good ol' terra firma.

"Please hurry, Nat. I'm really scared."

Brooke's fear gave her the courage to hurry. Trying to put the disturbing noise out of her mind, she reached for the end of the branch again, working to get the camera in place as quickly as she could. The noise could have been a machine, but it hadn't sounded mechanical. It had sounded like an animal. A *roaring* animal. Remembering the eerie howls that had foretold the beginning of the end at Dyatlov, Nat swore under her breath at her trembling hands.

Steady, steady. Don't fuck this up.

She wasn't sure she'd be able to host a podcast again, but maybe she could write a blog. Something that would put a bit more space between her and her followers. A clear photo of Bigfoot, even infrared, would launch a blog in a big way. Or she could sell it to another publication. Either way, she couldn't afford any mistakes. The money Riley was paying her would keep the wolf from the door for a while, but all too soon, she'd return to check-bouncing territory.

"Nat, something's coming."

She was about to ask what Brooke meant when she heard it herself—growling. Scanning the yard from her vantage point, she saw a section of the forest swaying as a large animal passed between the trees. "Run for the house, Brooke."

"Come down," Brooke begged, her voice thin and shrill. "Please, Nat."

Before Nat could tell the girl to get her ass in the house, another roar shattered the air. The tree branch thrummed underneath her. *Jesus Christ.*

Brooke shrieked.

Could she get down the tree and safely into the house before whatever it was got to her? Or was it safer to stay up here?

"Nat," Brooke screamed as the front door flew open.

"Brooke, get in here right now," Riley hollered, her eyes wild. "Run!"

"Nat's in the tree. I don't want to leave her."

Nat risked a look down to see the girl standing far below her, hesitating. Judging by how the trees were moving, the creature was almost at the edge of the forest. It wouldn't be long now, seconds at the most. Brooke was running out of time.

"I'll be safer up here. *Go.*" She added her voice to Riley's. Now both women were screaming at the girl to run for the house. Brooke stared at Nat, and then looked back at her mother, and Nat saw the problem. The girl was literally paralyzed with fear. She couldn't move.

"Shit."

She could see something crest the trees now, something dark—and huge. If it was a Sasquatch, it was walking in a crouch. It could have been a bear, which wasn't much more comforting.

Another roar—this one felt like a knife had been driven through her eardrums. She could see Riley was screaming, but she couldn't hear her. Swearing, Nat descended the tree as fast as she could, the bark tearing at her skin and jeans as she half-slid, half-climbed down its length. Her heart banged against her chest so hard it was painful. She'd never forgive herself if something happened to Brooke.

The next roar was close, way too close. Brooke clapped her hands over her ears, her mouth open in a shriek as Nat grabbed her. The girl was too big to carry, but adrenalin gave her strength, and she swung Brooke into her arms and ran like the devil was after her.

Riley reappeared in the doorway with a shotgun.

What the hell is she doing? No, you dumb bitch. You're going to get us killed.

The woman fired a warning blast into the air, startling Nat so much she nearly lost her grip on the girl.

Only a few feet more. Go, go, go!

Something pulled on her jacket, and Brooke screamed again, effectively deafening her. Nat was close enough to the house to set Brooke down, pushing the girl at her mother. Thankfully, Riley had regained her sanity enough to reach for her daughter and pull her inside. The door slammed shut, but two anxious faces at the window reassured her she hadn't been abandoned. Not yet.

Hot breath ruffled her hair as the creature snorted. It had a firm hold on her jacket, and Nat flung her arms out, helpless to stop the momentum as the creature yanked her back.

The door opened. "Get down, Nat." The shotgun was too close to home.

The thing holding Nat's jacket snarled. Another strong tug. "You're making it angry. Go back inside, please." Tears ran freely over her face; her bladder felt strangely weak. So this was it. After everything she'd survived, she was going to die here in Oregon. Life was strange.

Another growl.

Riley fired, the blast of the shotgun excruciatingly loud. Heat flashed past her face as the bullet hit its target behind her. The pressure on her jacket eased enough that Nat tore free of it, sprinting for the house.

"Go, go, *go*." She pushed Riley ahead of her and flung herself inside. Brooke slammed the door behind them.

Growling and huffing, the creature slammed into the door, but the wood held. Brooke wailed, and Nat went to comfort her while Riley stood ready with the gun. The next assault on the door was more halfhearted, and finally, the creature gave up.

"Nat, you're bleeding." Brooke pointed to Nat's hands, which were a gory mess.

"Guess I messed them up getting down the tree. Are you okay?"

Brooke nodded, but a sharp odor told Nat how scared the girl had been. She'd wet herself.

"Are you both all right?" Riley set the gun down by the door and wrapped her arms around her daughter, pulling her in for a hug. "I thought I was going to lose you. Why didn't you run?"

"I—I couldn't move. I was too scared." The girl wiped her eyes, squirming a little in her mom's crushing embrace.

Riley looked at Nat over the top of her daughter's head. "You probably saved her life. Thank you."

Was there some recrimination among the gratitude? After all, if it hadn't been for her, Brooke wouldn't have been out there in the first place.

"No worries. I'm glad everyone's okay. Well, besides my jacket." She paused before asking the question, not entirely sure she wanted to know. "What was it?"

A nervous smile trembled on Riley's lips. "A bear. The biggest black bear I've ever seen. It was enormous. You're lucky it didn't have a better hold on you."

Nat sank to the floor, stunned. *A bear?* That didn't seem right. Ordinarily black bears were afraid of people. Unless they were starving, sick, or feeling threatened, they avoided humans.

If the bear had been brave enough to attack them, why was she alive? Bears were stronger and faster. It could have knocked them both down and mauled them. *Why didn't it?*

Brooke broke free of her mother and ran to Nat, enveloping her in a fierce hug. "I was so scared. I thought you were dead."

She held the girl a moment, smoothing her hair. "Me too, kid. Me too."

Riley watched them with a strange expression before clearing her throat. "Brooke, why don't you go change, sweet pea? And can you bring me the First Aid kit so I can fix Nat's hands?"

Now that the adrenalin was wearing off, Nat's skinned palms were howling. Still, she knew how much worse it could have been. Imagining a bear's jaws closing around her skull, splitting it like an overripe melon, made her nauseous.

Brooke glanced at the women with a wary expression as she left the room. That kid was too smart for her own good. She knew something was up.

Nat wasn't surprised when Riley turned on her the second her daughter was gone, but that didn't keep her from being disappointed.

"What exactly were you thinking, leaving her unsupervised?" Riley demanded. "She could have been killed."

Though she knew there was no point in arguing when the woman was this upset, Nat couldn't stop herself from protesting. "She wasn't unsupervised. She was helping me."

"Helping you with what? What on earth were you doing out there? One minute, I think my daughter's safe in her bedroom, and the next I hear her screaming, you're in a tree, and the biggest bear I've ever seen is about to kill my child."

Nat looked at the hallway where Brooke had disappeared, hoping against hope the girl hadn't heard her mother. "Let's keep it down, Riley, please. I don't want to frighten Brooke more than she already is."

"It's a pity you didn't think of that before you nearly got her killed."

"Wait a second. Not that long ago, you were thanking me for saving her life. So which is it?"

"It feels damn strange, thanking someone for getting your child out of a bind she never should have been in in the first place. You *know* there's something out there, something dangerous. What the hell were you thinking?"

Nat took what she hoped would be a few calming breaths before responding. It wouldn't help anyone, least of all Brooke, if she and Riley started screaming at each other. "I thought the creature visited after dark, and that it would be good to have some photographic evidence, so Jason would be assured of your sanity once and for all. I made the mistake of letting Brooke come with me. She was bored and wanted to help. I'm sorry. It won't happen again."

She could feel the tension dissipate with her apology. Riley didn't look happy, but she relaxed slightly, leaning back in her chair. Nat no longer worried the other woman would try to throttle her.

Even though what had happened outside was no one's fault, except perhaps the bear's, apologizing cost her nothing but a little pride. She didn't have children, but she could imagine how protective she'd be if she did. She couldn't fault Riley for acting irrational—the woman had been scared out of her mind.

"Photographic evidence?" Riley asked. Nat could tell she was intrigued in spite of herself.

"I've rigged a motion-sensitive infrared camera outside the kitchen window. If all goes well, we should soon have some pics of your creature. Or, at the very least, of a big, angry-ass bear."

The corners of Riley's mouth twitched. "Christ, I don't think I've ever been that scared."

"Me neither," Nat said, though of course she had been. There were worse things in the world than angry bears, and she hoped Riley and her daughter would never come across them.

"Are you two done fighting now?" Brooke reappeared in a pair of fleece pajama pants festooned with stars. They looked so comfortable, Nat wished she had a pair of her own. The girl handed the First Aid kit to her mother, who rubbed her back.

"We weren't fighting, honey. Mommy was scared, that's all."

"I know, but it wasn't Nat's fault. I *made* her take me with her. Right, Nat?"

Nat tried her best to keep from smiling at the girl's obvious efforts to protect her. "You *were* pretty persuasive, but I was the adult in the situation, and I shouldn't have let you come. It was too dangerous."

"Since when?" Brooke flung herself into a chair. "Now I'm not allowed to play outside? In broad daylight?"

Nat looked at Riley across the table, and she recognized the mother's silent plea for help. Mothers were often considered overprotective, but the cool new house guest would be listened to. "I'm afraid not. Not until we find out what's going on out there."

The girl rolled her eyes. "Seriously? It was a *bear*. We live in the woods, for Pete's sake. A bear can show up at any fricking time."

"Brooke, watch your language," Riley said, but she sounded weary, as if her heart wasn't in it.

"Sorry, but I think it's silly. I can't stay cooped up in the house all the time. You're the one who always wants me to spend more time outside." Brooke's lower lip protruded, and for a moment Nat was tempted to repeat her grandmother's warning about faces freezing in unpleasant expressions. She decided against it. It probably wouldn't have worked any better on Brooke than it had on her.

"Honey, what do you think would have happened if Nat hadn't been there? Or if you'd both been a second or two slower getting inside?" Riley's voice cracked. "I don't mean to scare you, but we're all going to have to be more careful for the next little while. Nat too."

Whenever her therapist had admonished her about taking care of herself, Nat had dismissed the scolding with a flippant, "Who wants to live, anyway?" Without Andrew, without the career she'd loved, nothing had meaning anymore.

But now, sitting at this kitchen table with her hands screaming bloody murder, Nat realized something shocking. For the first time since Dyatlov Pass, she actually wanted to live.

CHAPTER SIX

As every mother knows, the best antidote to a near-death experience is pizza. Calling Domino's wasn't an option in the Oregon wilderness, so Riley made her own, whipping up a batch of whole-wheat pizza dough with impressive speed.

"This way, we each get to make our own," she explained. "Brooke loves it. I hope you like pizza?"

Nat downed her third cola of the night, having found the sugar-and-caffeine combination to be an okay, if unsatisfying, replacement for her usual beverage of choice. "Who doesn't?"

"We've developed our own little rituals for when Jason is out of town." Riley patted each lump of dough into a ball before covering them with a towel. "We call them Girls' Nights: something fun for dinner, followed by a movie. It makes it a bit easier to be on our own."

"Sounds like a great idea," Nat said, thinking for the hundredth time since she'd met the Tanners how different parents were now. Though strict when she needed to be, Riley obviously valued being her daughter's friend. Nat couldn't imagine sharing something as wholesome as pizza night with her own mother. Bourbon-and-cigarette night, maybe. An entirely different kind of family bonding.

Riley smiled at her, seeming completely recovered from the incident that afternoon. Opening the fridge, she retrieved another can of soda for Nat without being asked. "And now we have another girl joining us. Brooke is so happy you're here. She's always wanted a big sister, another woman she could look up to."

Not for the first time, Nat wished she were someone else. A "normal" woman who'd wanted to get married and have a family and a nice, stable career. Maybe someone who made pizza from scratch occasionally, or at least had Domino's on speed dial. She would have loved to play happy families with Riley and her daughter, but that's not why she was there.

"I'll gladly have dinner with you, but if it's all right, I'll sit out the movie. I should stay in here, keep an eye on things." Nat nodded toward the kitchen window, noticing with unease how dark it was getting. It wasn't like her to choose her words with care, but she'd done her best. Though she was still getting to know them, she liked Brooke. She liked Riley, though she didn't always agree with her. The last thing she wanted to do was hurt their feelings.

Riley's smile faltered as she got herself a beer. "Of course. You're right—we should stay here."

"No, no—please don't change your plans. It's best if you and Brooke do what you've always done. I suspect this creature is familiar with your routine. If it gets the sense we're waiting for it, it might not come, and that's the last thing we want."

"Really? I'd be thrilled if it decided to darken someone else's doorstep and leave us alone." She drank from the bottle, wiping the foam from her lips. Nat's mouth watered, and she looked away, pretending to be fascinated with the view.

"That would be ideal, but my fear is it wouldn't be permanent, and once I was back in California and you two were here by yourself, it would start all over again."

At least Jason had repaired the window before he'd left. Extra-strong, triple-pane glass, he'd said, cursing over how much it had cost. Nat could see how much he'd wanted to stay, to make the creature pay for the cracked window with a bullet in its brain. But not Nat. This one she wanted alive, if possible.

Now we know snowmen do exist.

She shook her head in an effort to clear it. This wasn't a snowman, and they weren't in Russia. And she wasn't going to watch anyone else die. Not again, not here.

A touch on her hand made her jump as if she'd been shocked. Riley was watching her with concern. "Are you okay? I feel like I lost you there for a minute."

"Yeah, I'm fine." Nat ran her hand through her hair and tried to sound reassuring. "Sorry, must be the excitement of this afternoon. What were you saying?"

"I was saying it's not going to be easy to convince Brooke. If you're out here, she'll want to stay here too." Riley's expression held a wistfulness that Nat understood—mothers, no matter how cool, could never be as cool as a mysterious house guest. She wanted to reassure Riley that she was the flavor of the week, that within days of her leaving,

Brooke would forget all about her, but she didn't want to sound patronizing.

"Well, we'll just have to explain how important it is. I'll help. No movie night, no Sasquatch." Nat hoped she sounded more confident than she felt. Privately, she was beginning to have her doubts. Was it a Sasquatch? What Riley had described certainly sounded humanoid, but even she hadn't gotten a good look at it. The bear's odd behavior that afternoon bothered Nat. What if there was some kind of virus or disease affecting the local wildlife? Something strong enough to make bears go mad and ignore their natural instincts?

"I don't mean to cop out, but is it all right if I let you do most of the convincing?" Riley focused on the label she'd begun peeling off the bottle of beer, looking sheepish. "I have a feeling she's more likely to listen to you in this case than me. After all, you're the expert."

Nat stifled her natural impulse to disagree. Riley needed her to be an expert, so an expert she would be. When it came down to it, she'd had more experience than most with so-called unnatural creatures. She guessed that qualified her more than any degree could. "Sure." An uncomfortable heaviness had settled over the room, which had felt light and cheery moments before. In an effort to change the subject, she asked, "Whatcha watching tonight?"

Riley shrugged, finishing her beer. "Tonight is Brooke's choice. Which probably means we'll have to have yet another talk about appropriate dress for preteens, and how no one really has breasts like that."

Nat choked on a laugh, narrowly avoiding filling her nasal passages with cola. "That bad?"

"Worse." Riley made a face. "The teen movies from my day weren't perfect by any means, but at least the kids looked like kids."

"Even though they were thirty."

She grinned, tipping her beer at Nat. "True. But as long as they were cute, what did we care?"

* * *

Riley knew her daughter well. As predicted, she wasn't happy about being relegated to the living room while Nat got to do the Sasquatch hunting alone.

"Are you kidding me? I'd trade places with you in a heartbeat. I'd much rather be watching a movie and eating popcorn than sitting out here waiting for something that might not happen." Nat wasn't lying, either. She would have gladly swapped with Brooke, but Riley hadn't paid her to be one of the girls. She'd hired her as a creature exterminator, so that's what she would be.

Thankfully it didn't take much convincing. Brooke obviously wasn't thrilled about it, but she gave in without a lot of fuss. It was almost enough to make Nat think having a kid could have been fun.

As the Tanner females adjourned to the living room, Nat felt strangely abandoned. A drink or five could have helped ease the isolation, but it wouldn't have done much for her creature-hunting skills.

The kitchen was cold, as if Brooke and Riley had taken the warmth with them. She could hear the murmur of the TV from the other room, followed by Brooke's laughter. Nat shivered, pulling on a sweater Riley had lent her. It was a navy cardigan, prim and functional, the type of thing she'd ordinarily never wear. Turning off the lights made her feel even more alone. Set free from the burden of social niceties, her mind began to misbehave.

What the hell am I doing, sitting in the dark in some stranger's kitchen, waiting for a Sasquatch? I must be out of my fucking gourd.

Then she remembered her shame when Kathy had told her about the bounced checks.

Right. Knew there had to be a reason.

Stretching out with her feet on the chair in front of her, Nat hummed the tune to an eighties pop song while she waited.

A loud thump from the living room brought her song to an abrupt end. She stiffened, her nerves on high alert. "Everything okay in there?"

The next thump was louder. The floor vibrated under her feet. From the other room, a shrill scream. *Brooke.*

"Jesus Christ." Nat swore under her breath as she ran into the living room, stumbling in the dark.

Riley and her daughter clung to each other, their backs pressed against the sofa as if by a centrifugal force. Their faces were drained of color, their eyes wide and strained. Outside the window, something stared back.

Something with glowing yellow eyes.

Nat's stomach dropped. She'd seen those eyes before. She knew the creature attached to them had no mercy, would rip the three of them apart with no hesitation, no remorse.

"The gun," she said through clenched teeth, as if the creature could lip read. Maybe it could. The things she'd faced in Russia had easily predicted her team's actions, remaining one step ahead.

When Riley didn't respond, Nat risked diverting her attention. "Riley, where's the goddamn gun?"

"It's in the gun safe. I thought you didn't want it."

In an irrational moment, Nat wanted to smack her. "Obviously I've changed my mind. Go get it *now*."

Brooke clung to her mother as Riley tried to leave, reverting back to her true age. "Mommy, don't go. I'm scared."

"I'll stay with her. Hurry." Yanking Riley away from Brooke's grasp, Nat gave her a little shove for good measure, never taking her eyes off the creature. It blinked, slowly. Why did she get the feeling it was amused, that it was thoroughly enjoying the show they were putting on?

What's taking so fucking long? Jesus Christ, Riley. Of all the times to be safety conscious.

Finally the woman returned with the gun. "It-it's not loaded."

"Where are the shells?" Nat was yelling now. What good was a gun without bullets? Where was the brave woman who'd charged outdoors, armed to the teeth, to defend her family?

"I-I'm sorry. I didn't think you'd want..." Riley fumbled with the stock, retrieving shells from her pockets. Seeing how her hands were trembling, Nat took the shotgun from her and loaded it herself. As she hefted the weapon in her arms, she sneered at the creature outside the window.

"Go ahead and stare, motherfucker. It's going to be the last thing you ever do."

She headed to the kitchen and the front door, with Riley and Brooke hollering after her, begging her not to go. Nat barely heard them. All she could think of was Andrew and the horrible way he'd died on that godforsaken mountain. Her blood roared in her ears, matching her rage.

These monsters had taken her best friend, ripped him apart for no reason. No one deserved to die like that. Being blown apart by a shotgun was a merciful act in comparison.

It was unnervingly dark outside, the kind of darkness only country folk knew. The creature would have the advantage, but at that moment, Nat didn't care. That fucker had killed Andrew, and she was going to make it pay.

Charging around the side of the house, shotgun poised to fire, she expected to encounter the creature as soon as she cleared the corner. Light spilled from the picture window, coloring the grass a sickly yellow, but there was no beast, no towering monster of death. Nat looked inside and saw Riley and Brooke staring at her, gesturing wildly at her to come in where it was safe. That was a laugh. Nothing was safe. This thing could break through their precious triple-pane glass as if it were cellophane.

"Not so brave anymore, are you?" Nat spat on the ground. "Show yourself now, you fucker."

Silence descended upon her, as heavy as the darkness had been seconds earlier. One of the Tanners must have muted the television. Nat could hear the thud of her own heart, louder than a drumbeat in her ears.

Eyes narrowing, she squinted into the night, panning the shotgun over the landscape, willing the creature to move. The slightest flicker, a wink of gold, and she'd fire. She'd do it for Andrew. For Igor. For her team, the ones that had stupidly trusted her and gotten themselves killed for their troubles.

Brooke screamed so loudly Nat could hear it through the glass.

Why is she calling me? For fuck's sake, I'm bus—

Focused on the women she'd left behind, Nat had forgotten to watch her back. She was unconscious before she hit the ground.

Fade to black.

CHAPTER SEVEN

It happened so fast.

One second it was nowhere to be seen, and the next, it was striking Nat with such force Riley was sure it had killed her. As the woman crumpled to the ground, Riley felt her own inertia break.

"Mom, no!" Brooke wailed, her face red and tear streaked. Riley hated to increase her little girl's suffering, but she couldn't leave Nat out there to die. Before she could think better of it, she pounded on the glass.

"Hey! You get the hell away from her. Leave her alone."

The creature bared its teeth in a sick parody of a grin. She could see it better now—the shaggy dark hair that covered its face, its wide nose and those terrible yellow eyes, glowing like a crematorium. This wasn't Bigfoot—this was something out of a psychotic's nightmare.

Watching her, it slowly stretched one of its arms toward Nat, much like a cat about to knock a glass off the counter, daring her to do something about it. Brooke grabbed her arm, holding on for dear life.

"No, Mom, please. Please don't go out there."

With a ruthlessness born of desperation, Riley tore out of her grasp. "If I don't, she'll die." Understanding full well that Nat was probably already dead, and wishing she'd kept her gun, she hurried to the kitchen and pulled the biggest knife from the butcher block. She'd had a great pitching arm back in the day; maybe she'd get lucky.

The creature didn't bother to hide from her as it had from Nat. It was there, waiting, when she rounded the corner. The sound of its breathing made her hands shake. Riley tightened her grip on the knife.

For a moment, time stopped as they stared at each other. The creature was so much bigger than she'd imagined, towering over her, its massive shoulders rising to its ears with every breath. It was *panting*. Could it be as afraid of them as they were of it? But no, that was ridiculous. A creature this gigantic had nothing to fear from them.

Eying her, it reached for Nat again. Riley brandished the knife, trying her best to appear intimidating. "Leave her alone. Don't you touch her."

She'd gotten its attention. It growled, low in its throat, and dropped into a crouch, retrieving something from the ground. *The gun.* As her heart fluttered into her throat, making it difficult to breathe, the creature bent the stock of the gun in half.

Tossing the twisted metal to the ground, it melted into the night, vanishing as completely as if it had never been there at all.

There wasn't time to question whether or not it had actually left. Riley rushed to Nat, dropping to her knees, terrified at what she would find.

She cried out in relief when she heard Nat breathe. Pressing her fingers to the woman's neck, she was comforted to feel a strong pulse. Nat's skin was cold, and she had blood on her forehead, but she was *alive.*

Riley knew the rules. You didn't move someone who'd suffered a head injury, but she'd be damned if she was leaving Nat out here. Supporting the woman's head as best she could, she struggled to lift her. Nat was smaller, but surprisingly heavy. Gritting her teeth, she staggered into a standing position, barely managing to bring Nat along with her. Thankfully the house was close enough to lean against, and Riley did, fighting to catch her breath.

Mercifully, Brooke appeared, lifting one of Nat's arms and putting it across her shoulders.

"Watch her head," Riley said, overwhelmed with relief. "Don't let it get jostled too much."

Praying they weren't doing more damage, Riley used her daughter's help to half-drag, half-lift Nat around the side of the house and inside. Brooke slammed the door behind them and locked it.

"Is—is she going to be okay, Mom?"

As much as she believed in honesty, there were times when a white lie was called for. "I think so. I think she's just unconscious. Let's put her on my bed, okay?"

Riley's mind raced as they muscled Nat's deadweight to the master bedroom. The nearest hospital was miles away.

Should she risk trying to lift the woman into her SUV? Or call for an ambulance? What if that thing was still out there and it attacked, killing them or anyone she called for help?

It could have killed you tonight, but it didn't.

They eased Nat's head onto the pillow, and then worked together to lift her legs on to the mattress. Now that the immediate crisis had passed, Riley noticed her T-shirt was covered with blood—Nat's blood. The woman's head injury must be worse than it had looked outside.

"Get the First Aid kit and my phone, Brooke."

Her daughter scurried out of the room. When this was over, Riley would have to remember to praise her, to tell her how well she'd reacted in an emergency. Her heart ached with guilt over what she was putting her daughter through. Why hadn't she asked more questions before she'd bought this place? She'd known Rod was hiding something when he'd shown her the house. He'd acted so evasive. Why hadn't she pressed him for answers?

Because you wanted this house. You didn't want anyone to talk you out of it.

When Brooke handed her the phone, the 9-1-1 operator was already on the line, sounding incredibly bored. Perhaps that was part of their training, how they kept people calm, but Riley found it irritating.

"What's your emergency?" the woman drawled, as if she didn't care one way or another.

"My—friend. She fell, and I think she hurt her head. There's a lot of blood."

The woman's interest did not sound piqued. "Where did she fall?"

"Outside our house. What I want to know is, should I drive—"

"Just a minute, ma'am. I need more information. How did she fall?"

A creature out of a horror movie clubbed her over the head. "I-I'm not sure. By the time I got there, she was on the ground, bleeding."

"So you're telling me you don't know how the incident occurred?" The operator sounded suspicious. Riley thought about the true-crime documentaries she'd watched, where they always played the recording of the 9-1-1 call. Would *this* be released to public scrutiny one day? Would people judge her lack of emotion, her hesitancy, and think *she'd* done this to Nat?

"No, but I'm wondering if I should bring her to the hospital. She's lost a lot of blood."

"Never move someone with a head injury, ma'am. I'll send an ambulance. What's your address?"

As she cradled the phone with her shoulder, Riley used gauze from the kit to staunch the bleeding from Nat's head wound. What if she'd made it worse by moving her? But what was she supposed to have done, waited for the creature to return and kill her?

"We're out of town. It's pretty far…"

"Address, ma'am."

She gave the woman her address and hung up, relieved that she wouldn't have to wrestle Nat into the SUV with only her ten-year-old daughter to help. Brooke's pupils were dilated. Her little face was pale and streaked with blood. Sometimes Riley forgot how young her daughter was. She was such an old soul.

"Are they coming?" Brooke asked, her voice cracking.

"Yes. But we have to be patient, and help Nat as much as we can. You've been very brave, sweetheart. Thanks for all your help."

Brooke sank onto the edge of the bed. "What if she dies?"

"She won't, honey," Riley said, though she'd been fearing the same. The gauze had turned red quickly—*too* quickly. Hating that she had to do this, understanding that it went against everything she'd tried to teach her daughter, she turned to Brooke with a sigh. "In the meantime, we should get our story straight."

"Story?"

Brooke's vacant expression spooked her. She wondered if her child was going into shock. Taking her daughter's hand in hers, she was startled by how cold it was. The girl's skin was like ice.

"They're going to want to hear how Nat got hurt. You heard me tell the lady I didn't see her fall, right?" Brooke nodded with all the emotion of a mechanical doll. "Well, you should say the same. Do you think you could do that?"

Her daughter frowned. "B-but it's a lie. We saw what happened. Bigfoot hit her."

Great. She could imagine how a paramedic would react to *that* story. It would be right up there with, "A dingo stole my baby," but only slightly less believable.

"We can't say it was Bigfoot. We don't really know *what* it was. Nat might have known, but we can't exactly ask her right now, can we?"

Brooke's face tightened into a stubborn expression Riley had seen before. This wasn't going to go well. As much as she admired her child's sense of right and wrong, she wished the girl was old enough to understand the world wasn't black or white, but many shades of grey.

"It *was* Bigfoot. I saw him."

"I know what you think you saw, sweetie, but—"

"I don't *think* I saw it. I *did* see it." Brooke's indignation had chased away any trace of shock. She glared at her mother. "It was real."

"I realize that, but the thing is…the thing is, if we tell anyone but Daddy that Bigfoot hurt Nat, they're not going to believe us. They might even think we're crazy."

Brooke's forehead furrowed. "But why wouldn't they believe us when we're telling the truth?"

"A lot of people think Bigfoot is like ghosts or UFOs. They don't think it's real. They might think *we* hurt Nat and made up the Bigfoot story to cover it up." Her daughter's expression darkened even further. "But we'd never hurt Nat."

"I know that, and you know that, but the people at the hospital don't. Sometimes bad people hurt others and make up big stories to cover it, so they'll think that's what we're doing."

"But if we lie, isn't that what we're doing? Remember when I told cousin Tammy that I was friends with Beyoncé? It was just a story—Tammy knew it wasn't the truth, but you and Dad still got mad at me. You said I shouldn't tell lies for any reason, even if I didn't mean for her to believe it."

Shit. Brooke was right—they *had* said that. Tammy's mother had laughed when she'd heard the story from her own daughter, but Riley had been mortified. That embarrassment had resulted in a teeny bit of overreaction, and the lesson had stuck. Her daughter had definitely gotten the message that lying was a Very Bad Thing.

But maybe they wouldn't be questioned. She had watched too many crime shows. Her friend had fallen, Riley hadn't seen the accident, no big deal. It's not like the police were going to show up and interrogate her and Brooke.

But what if they did? If worse came to worst, and she said she hadn't seen the accident, and her ten-year-old daughter claimed Bigfoot was responsible, what then? No matter how mature and responsible Brooke was, she was a child. Riley could picture a cop ruffling her daughter's hair as he laughed and said what a big imagination she had. There was nothing to worry about.

Then why was she so damn scared?

* * *

It took the paramedics about half an hour to arrive, which was better than she could have hoped, but it felt like forever. Nat's wound had exhausted the First Aid kit's supply of gauze by then, so they'd moved on to towels.

A man with caramel-colored skin and warm brown eyes gently moved her out of the way and hurried to her bedroom once she indicated where Nat was.

"Miss?" He lifted Nat's eyelids, checking her pupils with a small light. Nat didn't so much as moan. As he moved the sodden towel to examine the wound, Riley saw his face change. He didn't look friendly anymore. "How did this happen?"

Brooke huddled behind her, holding on to the waistband of her jeans, but thankfully she kept her mouth shut. "She had an accident. I heard her scream, and then I heard a thud, so I ran outside and found her lying on the ground."

Then Riley remembered the camera, and it was like a gift from God. "She was climbing a tree to set up her camera equipment, and I'm guessing she lost her balance."

The man gave her a look that could have frozen lava. "You *moved* her?"

"I know you're not supposed to, but there's a lot of wild animals around here and it was getting cold. It didn't seem safe to stay out there. And I didn't realize how badly she was hurt until we got her inside."

The medic shifted his attention to his partner, who had slipped into the room as silently as a shadow, though she was large and broad, with shoulders that spoke of power. "We're gonna need the stretcher."

With a curt nod, she was gone again. The paramedic spoke into his radio. "We've got a serious head injury, blood loss, possible skull fracture. Prepare the ER."

"You think her skull is fractured?" Riley shivered, feeling like she'd been plunged into ice water. She'd known Nat was injured enough to go to the hospital, but what if she died? How could she live with herself, knowing she'd caused an innocent woman's death?

Before the paramedic could answer, his partner burst into the room with the stretcher. She ushered Riley and her daughter to the side so they wouldn't be in the way as the paramedics fastened a surgical collar around Nat's neck and lifted her onto the stretcher, covering her with a blanket and strapping her in. Riley could only see a tuft of Nat's hair, tinged strawberry with her blood, as the paramedics wheeled her out of the room.

"Do you know her blood type?" the man called back to her, and she felt helpless as she told him no. She hardly knew Nat at all, let alone her medical stats.

As Riley followed the medics outside, an arm around her daughter, she hoped the creature was long gone. *Please let us have suffered enough for one night.* Of course, it was Nat who was truly suffering. What if she didn't make it?

When the paramedics loaded the stretcher with her unconscious new friend into the back of the ambulance, Brooke couldn't hold her tongue any longer. "Can we come with you?" she asked in a voice so pitiful, it hurt Riley's heart.

The man hesitated, and then looked over at Riley. "Are you okay to drive?"

When she nodded, he said, "You and your mom can follow us in your car," before slamming the ambulance doors.

The crimson lights made the world bleed, but there were no sirens. There was no need for them on the quiet country roads.

Riley hadn't missed the recrimination in his eyes, but whether it was because she'd moved Nat or he blamed her for the injury, she couldn't say.

CHAPTER EIGHT

The doctor motioned Riley into his office, his face set in stern lines.

"Your friend wasn't hurt in a fall."

"No?" Riley asked, squeezing Brooke's hand until her daughter squeaked, willing her to keep quiet. Groggy and rumpled from their hours in the waiting room, they'd been close to falling asleep when the doctor had summoned them.

"No. She appears to have been attacked by an animal. My best guess is a bear."

"Really?" Riley turned to her daughter to prevent the doctor from seeing the relief on her face. "We had a problem with a bear earlier today—it went after my daughter, and God knows what would have happened if it hadn't been for Nat. Nat saved her life."

"That's a concern. We can't have bears wandering into people's yards and attacking them. I'll have to report this to the police."

"What makes you think it was a bear?" Riley asked, praying she wasn't pushing her luck.

The doctor glanced at Brooke before responding. "Perhaps we should discuss this privately."

Brooke's grip on her hand tightened, but Riley knew not everyone saw her daughter the way she did. Unusually mature or not, she was a child in the doctor's eyes. "Honey, why don't you take my purse and go get yourself a soda from the vending machine?"

"I'm not thirsty," Brooke said, pouting.

Riley gave her a warning look. "Then get a snack."

Her daughter made a big show of her disgust, sighing and moaning and dragging her feet, but she was smart enough to get when not to mess with her mother. Finally she left, shutting the door a little harder than required.

The doctor smiled. "They can be so precocious at that age."

Riley bristled. "She's normally great. This has been a tough night for her."

"Of course." He cleared his throat. "As I was saying, your friend's wound is fairly serious. The flesh was nearly flayed from the top of the skull, with evidence of what could only be claw marks. Due to the fracture, her brain was swelling. Thankfully, we managed to relieve the pressure without surgery, but if she'd gone too much longer without treatment, she would not have made it."

That sounded worse than Riley had suspected. "Is she going to be all right?"

"I hope so, but I have to be honest with you. Head injuries are complicated beasts. We're never quite sure what the long-term repercussions will be, but we always hope for the best and plan for the worst."

Riley braced herself. "And what is the worst, in this case?"

"We won't know until she regains consciousness, and perhaps not even then. For the present time, we're keeping her in an induced coma to allow her brain to heal as much as possible before we bring her back." He frowned, rubbing his chin. "I believe you told my staff you aren't sure how to reach her next of kin?"

"No. I hardly know her. I mean, I was *getting* to know her, but I met her a few days ago. I guess you would call us friendly acquaintances."

The doctor raised an eyebrow. "I thought she was staying at your house when the injury occurred?"

"She was…she *is*. But she's staying at our house to do some research. She's a…naturalist," Riley said. The one good thing about the long wait was that it had given her plenty of time to come up with a story. "She's interested in studying the local wildlife."

"Given what happened last night, perhaps it would be best if she considered another career. One of the nurses did find some identification that mentioned a podcast. *Nat's Mysterious Universe*, or something of that nature?"

Shit. "*Nat's Mysterious World*. She used to host a podcast, but she gave it up a long time ago." Riley hoped the fact it was the truth would steady her voice. "Now she's committed herself full time to science."

"I see. Let's hope her brain cooperates. She's going to be under for a while, so I suggest you take your daughter home, get some rest. We'll call you if anything changes."

It didn't feel right to abandon Nat, especially when Riley was the reason the woman had come to Oregon in the first place. But from what the doctor said, Nat wouldn't know if they were there or not, and Riley was dead on her feet. The idea of going home and collapsing for a few hours was irresistible.

"Are you sure there's nothing else we can do?"

"No, nothing, unless you have some magic way of calming her down."

"Calming her down? I thought she was in a coma."

"She is, but in spite of this, her blood pressure and heart rate remain high. She doesn't lie still, so we've had to resort to restraints. It's like she's fighting something off."

* * *

She seized Andrew's hands, clamping down with all her strength. His fingers tightened on hers, and she felt rather than heard her joints crack under the pressure. Rivulets of blood trickled across her skin from where his nails had cut her.

In spite of her efforts, the beast was stronger. Every time it pulled on Andrew's legs, they both flew forward across the snow. Her friend screamed.

"*Don't let it get me.*"

"I won't. Don't worry," she yelled over the creature's infernal howling, but it was impossible. Whenever she gained an inch, the monster took three. At any moment, it would stop playing this ludicrous game and kill them both.

A wizened man appeared beside them, startling her. His skin was like well-tanned leather, his face and chest streaked with gore. In horror, she watched as he pulled his coat open, revealing the hilt that protruded from his breastbone. Grinning maniacally, he grasped the knife with both hands and wrenched it from his body. It came free with a vile sucking sound, releasing a torrent of blood that splashed her face, warm and salty. Turning away from the man, she gagged.

He crouched beside her, putting the bloody weapon in her hand and closing her fingers around it. "Perhaps you can use this," he said in a voice that was more hiss than speech. "As I recall, you were quite good with it."

As she hollered at him to get away from her, to leave her alone, the creature jerked on Andrew's legs with more force than before. She felt her friend's grip loosen as he was taken from her, taken by that hateful thing with the hateful yellow eyes.

This time the inhuman howl came from her. Scrambling to her feet, fighting for purchase on the snow and ice, she swung the knife home, again and again, until there was nothing left but a ruin of flesh, bone, and brain matter.

Gasping, close to collapsing from exertion, she let the knife fall from her fingers. Now that the fight was over, she realized how cold she was, and her entire body began to shake as she fell to her knees on the snow, ice crystals digging into her snow pants.

Andrew's breathing didn't sound good. She'd never heard a person breathe that way before, like air passing through an enormous bellows. What if she lost him, after everything?

"Andrew?"

The silence remained, broken only by that strange wheezing. Wondering if he'd been hurt in the struggle, she dared to look.

Hateful yellow eyes looked back. The creature loomed above her, its labored breathing causing the sound that had made her skin crawl.

"*Andrew.*"

Her dearest friend was the ruin at her feet.

The gore-streaked man smiled.

CHAPTER NINE

Riley struggled to keep her eyes open on the drive home. She negotiated the abandoned country roads on autopilot, grateful that her chatty daughter was silent for a change. Ordinarily this would have worried her, but she didn't have the energy to get them home alive and hold up her end of a conversation.

The late-morning sun was breathtaking as it shone through the crimson, magenta, and pumpkin-hued leaves, but Riley was too exhausted to notice. Her weary eyes watered until she slipped on her sunglasses.

Unlike Brooke, her mind refused to be quieted. It went over and over every conversation she'd had with Nat, each measly bit of small talk. Had she mentioned any family, any significant other waiting for her at home? Riley couldn't remember Nat venturing into anything personal, and she'd never seen her text anyone. Still, she must have someone who would be worried about her. Somehow, she'd have to figure out a way to notify them. Decisions might need to be made about Nat's care, and she was hardly qualified to make them.

Her shoulders slumped with relief as she reached their driveway at last. They had another night ahead of them to worry about, a night without Jason *or* Nat, but not yet. First, sleep.

"Mom?"

It took a surprising amount of effort to make her lips form a reply. "Yes?"

"Look."

She followed Brooke's trembling finger to the devastation that had once been their front porch.

The door had been torn off its hinges. It hung askew, useless, like a child's loose tooth. Four deep gashes were scored in its wood—claw marks. The wicker patio furniture Riley had chosen with such care was in worse shape, most of it smashed to bits. Her eyes stung with tears.

"Why would it do this?" her daughter cried, and she had no answers—until she saw the window. Embedded in the glass, in the middle of a web of cracks, was Nat's infrared camera.

Wiping away her tears, she scanned the yard for any movement. Aside from the rustling of leaves in the wind, there was none.

"Follow me, and stay close. It could be nearby." *Or in the house*, but that thought was too horrible to vocalize. Their sanctuary had been violated, leaving her feeling naked and excruciatingly vulnerable.

She pushed open the door of the SUV, half-expecting something to rush her from behind. There was nothing but birdsong. The tranquil beauty of the day belied the disaster area before them. Hopping to the ground, her exhaustion was forgotten as her senses switched to high alert, straining to hear any unusual sound, see any motion.

Waiting until Brooke was beside her, her hands hooked into the waistband of her jeans again, Riley approached the house with caution.

"What's that smell?"

As soon as Brooke said it, Riley caught a whiff of it too. Something rancid and meaty, like a well-used outhouse. "I don't know."

Her footsteps quickened, but the smell got worse, not better, as they drew closer to the house. They discovered the source at the same time.

"Eew, gross," Brooke squealed.

Their savage neighbor had left them a present. In their demolished doorway waited a heaping pile of fragrant dung. Riley wrinkled her nose. "Lovely."

Stepping over the shit, she was relieved to find the creature had apparently been satisfied with ravaging the exterior of their home. There were no signs it had moved inside, but the warning was clear. Breaching their sanctuary was as easy as tearing a door off its hinges or breaking a window. They weren't safe here.

"Go pack a bag with everything you'll need for a night or two."

For once, Brooke did what she asked without question, running up the stairs two at a time. Riley hurried to her own room, wincing when she saw her blood-soaked bed. She had to reach Jason before he got home or he'd think a massacre had happened there.

Stepping around the debris of used gauze and bandage packs, she found a small suitcase under the bed and filled it with the basics. After a second of hesitation, she added her favorite family photo album, though this required removing a pair of jeans. Who could predict what the creature would do next? What if it destroyed their belongings? Or ripped the house apart?

As much as she hated to concede a battle, there was bravery and then there was stupidity. The creature had won this round. The best she could do was get her daughter someplace safe until her husband returned, and then they could regroup and figure out what was next.

But first, it was time for a long overdue phone call.

Carrying the suitcase, Riley made her way to the kitchen while she waited for him to pick up. Three rings, four. *Come on, you bastard, be there.*

"Silverwood Realty. Turning dreams into reality since 1974. Rod speaking."

"Rod? This is Riley Tanner."

There was a brief pause, allowing the real estate agent either to scan his memory banks for who she was, or to wonder why she'd called. "Why, good morning, Riley. What an unexpected pleasure. Beautiful day, isn't it?"

She gritted her teeth so hard her jaw ached. "I've seen better."

"Oh? I'm sorry to hear that. What can I do for you? I hope everything is all right with the house."

"Actually, it's not. I need the front door replaced."

"What a shame."

"I assume you know someone reputable in the area who could take care of it? We—we're going out of town for a few days, so I'd like you to handle the repairs, if you wouldn't mind."

Rod clicked his tongue, and Riley waited for him to deny her, to remind her this wasn't his job. She would have loved an excuse to blast him. "Things have been hopping around here lately, but for you, I'm sure I can handle it. Do you want the replacement to look like the original?"

"No. I want something stronger."

"Stronger? Riley, that door was top of the line, as strong as they come."

"It was still wood, with flimsy hinges. I want metal. Solid metal, like you'd find on a vault."

He paused again, and if it hadn't been for the sound of his breathing, she might have thought he'd hung up. "That...that could be quite expensive. The frame would need to be upgraded."

"I don't care. Text me the price before you confirm, but the cost is not my main concern." She pushed aside Jason's future reaction to the excessive bill. If that thing could get in their home, they'd have to move, and that would be far more expensive than replacing a door.

"All right, then. Consider it done. Always happy to help my loyal clients."

"Which leads me to my next question. I need to speak to the former owners." Riley's fingers ached, and she saw she had the phone in a death grip. Switching hands, she tried to relax. Taking her frustration out on her cell was hardly the way forward.

"Pardon me?"

"You heard me, Rod. The people who sold this place. I want their number."

She heard the agent's sharp intake of breath, and settled in for a fight. It was as she'd suspected. He wasn't going to make this easy.

"I can't do that, Riley."

"And why the hell not?"

"It's an invasion of their privacy, for starters. Any issues you have with the house, you can discuss with me."

She gripped the back of a kitchen chair, about to unleash every filthy word provided by her New York upbringing, when Brooke wandered into the room with her duffel bag, wide-eyed and pale. Fine. She'd keep the language PG, but that didn't mean she had to be civil. "I tried that, but you lied to me. So I want to talk to them."

"*Lied* to you? I did nothing of the kind."

Amazing how the greasy bastard managed to sound shocked. He was one hell of an actor, she'd give him that. "Cut the shit. I'm not in the mood."

"Look, I appreciate your business. And I'm happy to take care of the door repairs for you—that's not a problem. But just because you're a client gives you no right to speak to me that way."

"Maybe not, but being lied to does."

Rod huffed in her ear. "Perhaps you should tell me what this is all about."

"The *wildlife*, Rod? The local wildlife? You made it sound like these people had a case of city-folk vapors, wetting their drawers over owls and bears. I think we both know this is about a little more than wildlife."

"I'm sorry; I'm not following. Have you had bear problems?"

"No. Aside from the fact one almost tore my daughter to bits yesterday, the bears are fine." Riley patted Brooke's hand and shook her head to show she was exaggerating. "What I have are Sasquatch problems."

The other end of the line went silent for so long she wondered if he'd hung up on her. But no, he wouldn't dare. Not with the fine reputation of Silverwood Realty at stake. Finally, he cleared his throat.

"Come again?"

"Sasquatch. Bigfoot. At least one, but there could be more, for all I know—it's not like I've tagged them. They've been terrorizing me and my daughter, and now they've ripped apart my door and put my friend in the hospital. I want to know exactly what those people did to antagonize them, so I can undo it."

Another pause. "Mrs. Tanner, you're not well."

Holy Christ. He really didn't know. "You come take a look at my door, and tell me you think a fucking bear ripped it off its hinges." Catching herself, she patted Brooke's hand in apology again. Hopefully her daughter would give her swearing a pass in these interesting times. "Perhaps you think a bear threw an infrared camera through my kitchen window too. Completely natural bear behavior."

"Even if I did give you their number—which I'm not going to—if you were to call them up, ranting and raving about a Sasquatch, of all things, how long do you think it would take before they hung up?"

Riley felt her eyes narrow into slits. Too bad Rod wasn't here to benefit from her patented glare of death. The fucker deserved it. "They wouldn't hang up. Because they, more than anyone else, would know I'm telling the truth."

"I'd love to help you, and I would if I could, but I specifically promised the agent that if anything came up about the house after the sale, I would handle it. The owners wanted to leave this place, and everything about it, far behind them."

"Right there," she yelled, making Brooke jump. "Doesn't that tell you something? There's a reason they were in such a hurry to get out of here. No one is that scared of owls and bears, I don't care how sheltered they are."

"It's not for me to speculate. They weren't my clients, but I promised to honor their privacy, as I'm sure you'd want me to honor yours."

"I don't give a shit what you do with my privacy right now, Rod. Oh, and speaking of shit, Bigfoot left a big pile of it on the porch for you. Feel free to rub your face in it."

Riley ended the call, wishing for the good ol' days when you could slam a receiver down so hard the plastic cracked.

"Wow, Mom, I've never heard you so mad." Brooke stared at her with a combination of fear and respect.

"It pisses me off. I'm sorry for the things you heard, sweetheart. Mom should have controlled her temper. But I don't like being played for a fool, and especially not by him."

"So we can't talk to the people who lived here before?"

"Oh, we can talk to them. It just would have been easier if he'd agreed to help us out."

"But..." Brooke crinkled her nose. "If he wouldn't give you their names, how are we going to find them?"

She winked. "This is a small town, isn't it? If Rod won't tell me, there'll be plenty of people who will."

* * *

71

Nat was freezing, but rather than cursing the cold, she welcomed it. Lately she'd been feeling sensations of warmth, which scared her more than anything, as it was a warning rather than a welcome. Feeling warm meant she had hypothermia. It meant she was dying. After everything she'd been through, she'd take the cold over that. "Nat? Ms. McPherson, can you hear me?"

She blinked in surprise. Was Steve finally losing his mind? Of course she could hear him. It wasn't like their shelter was large. And why was he being so formal? He never called her Ms. McPherson.

"Do you think we're going to get out of here?" she asked.

He smiled, even though she could see how violently he was shaking. If the creatures didn't kill them, the cold soon would. "Yes. I wouldn't have gone to all this trouble otherwise."

"Sometimes I dream that I've escaped from here." She decided to confide in him, in spite of the fact she didn't trust him. They had no choice but to trust each other now. "I'm back in California, but everything is different."

"Sure it's different. You're fucking everything up—left, right, and center. You've turned into a train wreck, Nat. What happened to you? You used to be so strong."

Nat bristled, her shame and anger at Steve's rebuke making her forget about the cold for a moment. "How can you ask me that? You *know* what happened to me."

"It's no excuse for fucking up your life. People have survived worse than this and made something of themselves. You threw a pity party and gave up. If I'd known you were going to be such a wimp, I wouldn't have risked my ass to save your life."

"What are you talking about? I saved myself." Furious tears stung her eyes, but she refused to let them fall. Bad enough Steve could tell he was goading her. She wouldn't let him see her cry too. That would only confirm his low opinion of her.

"Yeah, right. Just like you saved Andrew. Some leader you are." Steve rolled his eyes and turned away from her.

"What happened to Andrew wasn't my fault. I'm not the one who killed him." She bit her lip hard, willing the tears to stop, but at the thought of her best friend, it was impossible.

"Oh yeah? Then why is his head in your lap?"

Startled, she looked down, screaming when she saw her friend's face staring back at her. Before she could push it away, it opened its eyes and spoke.

"Why did you let me die, Nat? I thought we were friends. Why did you kill me?"

Squeezing her eyes shut, she thrashed her arms and legs, frantic to escape, to get away from them both. "I didn't kill you. Leave me alone. Please, all of you, leave me alone!"

"Ms. McPherson?"

Nat opened her eyes to see an unfamiliar face looming over her. A female face. But that was impossible. All the other women were gone. Was this another ghost, come to taunt her and blame her? She shook her head. "No."

"You're not Ms. McPherson?"

"You know who I am. Stop playing dumb."

The woman smiled. "I see you haven't lost any of your spirit. Do you know where you are?"

"Why are you asking me these inane questions? I'm in Dyatlov, same as you."

The woman's forehead creased with concern. "You're in a hospital, Ms. McPherson. In Longview, Oregon."

Oregon? Nat's mind whirled, remembering Steven's admonishment that she was fucking everything up. Was this a part of it? Some critical test that she'd failed, and now she'd ended up in a hospital? It had to be a trick.

"I didn't kill Andrew, Lana. You have to realize that."

The woman looked even more confused. "My name is Pat. I think you've been dreaming. You've been in the hospital for a few days now, in a coma. Don't you remember what happened? A woman named Riley has been visiting you every day with her daughter. I think they're friends of yours? They'll be so happy to find out you're awake."

Before Nat could answer, a man nudged the woman out of view. "Do you remember what happened to you, Ms. McPherson?"

Who were these people, and why did they insist upon asking such ridiculous questions? How could anyone forget what she'd been through? She'd need a lobotomy, which had seemed more and more appealing lately. "It was the creature," she said, her tongue feeling thick and furry. She longed for water. If she were really in a hospital, they should have offered her water. It was obvious these people were lying, but fine, she'd play along. What else was there to do, other than wait to die?

"Which creature is that?" the man asked, as if he didn't know. As if anyone could forget those hideous yellow eyes, that stench.

"The ones who are killing us. They're hard to miss. Funny, but I never got the chance to ask their names."

Nat heard the woman's voice again. "It's too soon for this, officer. She's still delirious."

"Clearly," the man said, and his smugness irritated her. He reminded her of Steven, thinking he knew everything, thinking women were inferior beings who needed to be saved. Well, fuck that.

"I'm not delirious, and I'm not insane. Creatures attacked us and killed all our friends. If you don't believe me, ask Igor." Igor would tell the truth. The rest of them were lying sacks of shit. Her first mistake had been trusting them. But Igor—Igor was different.

"Who's Igor?" the man asked. At least he wasn't acting like he knew everything. That was a welcome change.

"I have no idea," the woman replied. "She's been having lots of violent nightmares—struggling, fighting something off. She must have had something traumatic happen in her past. Perhaps Igor was a part of it."

"Her skull was cracked. I'd say it's fairly obvious something traumatic happened."

Ah, the man's pomposity had returned. Nat had figured the humility was too good to last.

"The woman who came with her said she fell."

"Hell of an injury for a fall, don't you think? Ms. McPherson, can you tell me what happened?"

Annoyed, Nat tried to turn over so she couldn't see his stupid, knowing expression any longer, but her arms were strapped down. She had to satisfy herself with turning her head and closing her eyes again. "I'm done talking to you."

"Well, I'm not done talking to you. I'm going to find out what happened to you, and that's a promise. Creatures," the man said, and snorted. "Now that's one I haven't heard before."

Nat wanted to tell him to get bent, but wasn't willing to expend the energy. She felt so tired lately; it was probably the cold. Her body was shutting down, bit by bit, toe by toe. Maybe she should stop fighting so hard.

Maybe she should let herself die.

CHAPTER TEN

They began their search at the Longview Library. Riley wasn't sure why, exactly. She hadn't been inside a library in years, probably not since university. But if any place could be counted on to be a repository of old information, she figured it had to be a library.

"Remember," she told her daughter as they exited the SUV, "not a word about what we've seen. Otherwise, we'll end up in the hospital with Nat."

Nat. They hadn't visited her yet that day. Riley felt a twinge of guilt. When this was finished, they'd grab some lunch and then head to the hospital. The woman was in a coma; it's not like she was keeping track. But somehow knowing that didn't make her feel better. It was Riley's fault Nat had gotten hurt in the first place. The least she could do was keep her company.

As she'd expected, the library was silent, and close to deserted. A young woman with an unfortunate case of acne glared at them from the seating area. From the way she was curled up on the chair with a stack of books beside her, she'd been there a while. Riley had to stop herself from apologizing for disturbing her.

She waited at the checkout desk for a few minutes, tapping her fingernails against the polished wood, until the librarian appeared.

"Sorry, I was in the back and didn't hear you come in. Can I help you?"

"Yes. I'm looking for…" Riley hesitated. What *was* she looking for? "Do you have any town records?"

"What kind of records are you hoping for? We have a history of Longview that was written by a local teacher. It's quite good."

"Maybe that would help, but I'm more interested in the history of some of the local properties. Who lived there before, etcetera." Riley hoped she didn't sound like a stalker. Now that she was here, it was hard not to feel guilty, as if she was asking for information she had no right to.

"Which properties, specifically, are you interested in? Depending on the addresses, I might be able to help, but if it's anything recent, I suspect you'll have to go to the Town Hall."

Lowering her voice, Riley gave her address. There was a flicker of recognition in the woman's eyes, but it was there and gone so quickly it would have been easy to suspect she'd imagined it.

"N-no, I'm..." The librarian's voice cracked and she cleared her throat. "No, I'm sure we don't have anything for that address. You'll have to try the Town Hall."

"You must have something," Riley said, her curiosity aroused by the strange reaction. "Something about the people who built the house, maybe? Or the property itself?"

The woman straightened, her once-friendly face turning to stone. "No, I'm afraid I don't."

"1699 Forest Drive? That's the monster house," the girl sitting on the chair behind them yelled, prompting Brooke to huddle against her mother's side.

"Now, you shush, Clara. These people aren't interested in hearing your nonsense."

The girl rose, hands on hips. Riley was startled to see how tall she was. She had to have been six feet, and she had a formidable girth, as well, which was unkindly highlighted by her pleated skirt. "Don't you dare hush me like I'm crazy, Juliet. You know it's true as well as I do." She narrowed her eyes at Riley, and Brooke whimpered, clutching her mother's hand. "Why do you wanna know about the monster house?"

Riley was tempted to follow the librarian's example and tell this girl it was none of her business, but she suspected Clara might be the one person in town willing to take her seriously. "Because I live there."

The girl hooted. "You *bought* that place? You must be really dumb."

"Clara!" The librarian paled, looking horrified. "I'm so sorry. Clara has some...challenges. She doesn't always think before she speaks."

"It's okay. I *am* beginning to feel really dumb." Riley strived to sound warm and encouraging in the face of the girl's derision. The more she could find out, the better. "What do you know about my house, Clara?"

"I know it's full o' monsters, that's what. Monsters own that place, and always will. You might live there, but you'll never own it. It's theirs."

"What kind of monsters?"

Clara cocked her head to the side. "Why you here if you ain't seen them?"

Figuring that question was best left unanswered if she didn't want Juliet warning the town about her own "challenges," Riley tried again. "What kind of monsters?"

"Bigfoot, Sasquatch, the terrible ape." Clara pursed her lips and made a huffing noise, blowing her bangs off her broad forehead. "You ain't from around here, are you? Everyone knows Oregon is the home of the terrible ape."

"How many times do I have to tell you that's only a legend? It's a made-up story," Juliet said, with a world-weary sigh. "There's no such thing as Bigfoot."

Riley stifled the temptation to invite the woman over for dinner. Juliet would soon see how mythical her "legend" was. Instead, she decided to ignore the librarian and focus on the girl.

"Why do they own my house? What draws them there?"

Clara shrugged. "Who knows? Mebbe they're pissed that someone put a stupid ol' house in the forest. The forest is their real home, you know. That's where they hide. They don't like visitors. Anyone with any sense stays far away."

"I'm afraid you're being very rude, Clara. I'm so sorry," the librarian said to Riley. "Bigfoot is her favorite subject, and when she gets on a roll, she forgets her manners."

"Can you please stop talkin' about me like I'm not here?" Clara shouted. "I'm not dumb, you know. Or deaf."

"It's okay," Riley said. "I'm not offended. I'd like to hear what she has to say."

"See?" Clara said, chest puffing out in a caricature of pride. "Not everyone thinks I'm useless the way you do."

"I don't think you're useless. I never said that. I just find you very…tiring sometimes." The librarian leaned her head against her hand, looking every bit as exhausted as she sounded. Though Riley was grateful for the girl's honesty and outspokenness, she was glad she didn't have to deal with it daily.

Clara made that exasperated noise again. Riley suspected she made it a lot. "There ain't nothing tiring about me. I come here and I read books. That's what a library's *for*."

She did have a point, Riley thought. Better the girl was in here, reading, than out on the streets causing trouble. Juliet had no right to shame her. But before she could feel too sympathetic, Clara pointed at her.

"You need to move."

"Excuse me?"

"You need to move, lady, fast. The monsters will never let you have their house, and they won't stop till you're dead. Your only hope is to move away like the other people did."

Riley's interest was piqued. "Other people? What other people?"

Clara made a face. "You know, the Riordans. They didn't even say goodbye. Just hightailed it out of here like they was on fire."

"That's not nice. Honestly, I have no idea where you get your ideas," Juliet said.

"Ain't no need to get them from nowhere if they're true."

"I'd love to speak to the Riordans. Do you know where they went?" Riley mentally crossed her fingers, though she couldn't imagine anyone giving this bizarre child their forwarding address.

"Course I know. Everybody knows. They went to Phoenix. That's the name of the town. It's named after a bird that can survive fire. Have you heard of it?"

Riley nodded. "Yes, it's in Arizona."

"Now you be sounding like Juliet. Everybody knows it's in Arizona. I'm not dumb, you know."

"No, you're not. You're very smart, and you gave me the information I needed. Thank you, Clara." With a hand on her daughter's back, Riley ushered Brooke toward the door.

"Whatever," Clara said with a shrug, flopping down in her chair. "Just move, okay? We got enough problems around this place without cleaning up the mess they'll make of you if you stay."

* * *

"Do you think you'll be able to find them now, Mom?" Brooke asked once they were safely away from Clara.

"I hope so. It's hard to say. Phoenix is a big place." Riley wished she'd thought to get Clara to spell the last name. *Riordan*, she typed on her phone, hoping it was correct. "But at least it's a start. It's more than Rod was willing to give us."

"That girl was scary. I didn't like her." Brooke twisted her nose and shuddered theatrically, in case her words left any doubt.

"She was a little different, but that doesn't make her scary."

"A *little* different?" Now it was Brooke's turn to roll her eyes. "Get real, Mom."

"Okay, a lot different. Happy now? Remember what I taught you. There's nothing wrong with being different. Wouldn't the world be a boring place if we were all the same?"

"Better than being like her."

"Brooke, that's a horrible thing to say. That poor girl has a learning disability. She's probably had a tough life. You have no idea what she's gone through."

Brooke stared out the windshield. "Sorry. I still don't like her."

"You don't have to like her. Just…be kind."

"It's hardly like I was *mean* to her, Mom. I didn't say anything to her."

"You're being mean in your mind, and that counts just as much."

Her daughter gave her a dark look before turning back to the window. The cold shoulder. Clearly the discussion was over. Riley hoped her point had been made. While she was happy her daughter was pretty and smart and popular, she was determined Brooke wouldn't become one of those bullying girls who made fun of everyone else.

"Hungry?" she said, in an effort to change the subject. "I thought we'd stop for lunch before going to see Nat."

Brooke shrugged, not quite daring enough to avoid answering her mother entirely yet, but Riley knew that day was coming.

"Well, I'm starving. The hospital cafeteria it is." Riley made a more dramatic-than-called-for turn onto 42nd Street, knowing her daughter would feel it.

"Ugh, do we have to? Even their Jell-O is gross," Brooke whined, and Riley hid her smile. Nothing like the threat of hospital food to overcome the silent treatment.

The nurse stepped in front of her before she could reach Nat's room. "Ms…Tanner, is it?"

"Yes, I'm Riley Tanner. What's wrong?" Riley felt Brooke tense beside her, as they both braced themselves for bad news.

"Nothing's wrong. It's the opposite, actually. Your friend is awake. Woke up two hours ago. We tried to inform you, but couldn't get a response."

Automatically Riley checked her cell. It was dead. When was the last time she had charged it? Jason was probably frantic by now. "So she's okay?"

"It's too soon to say how much, or if any, long-term damage has been done. She does appear to be a bit confused. She keeps insisting she's in a place called Dyatlov. Does that mean anything to you?"

Riley tightened her grip on Brooke's hand. "Dyatlov Pass. It's in Russia. She had a…traumatic experience there."

The nurse's face relaxed. "I'm glad to hear it was a real experience, even though it wasn't pleasant. This means her memories are returning. Do you know how long ago this occurred?"

"Not too long. About a year ago, I think? Maybe a little longer." Riley struggled to remember what her friend June had told her, since Nat never talked about it.

"I'm hoping seeing you and your daughter will help her remember where she is and why. She may mistake you for someone else. If she does, gently correct her, but be careful not to show fear or too much concern," the nurse said.

"We can do that, can't we, Brooke?" Riley hugged her daughter about the shoulders. Brooke adored Nat. Perhaps seeing her awake at last would bring Brooke out of her current funk. Even chicken sliders hadn't helped, and sliders usually cured everything.

"Sure," Brooke said, but her eyes were wary. This was the first experience she'd had with sickness and hospitals. Keeping her arm around her daughter, Riley led the way into Nat's room.

Nat's head was bandaged, but her breathing tube had been removed. Some color had returned to her skin, which had taken on a yellowish hue the last time they had visited.

Instead of sleeping, she stared at the ceiling, her arms restrained by both wrists. Riley made a mental note to ask the nurse if they were necessary. It had to be horribly uncomfortable, and Nat was so wan and diminished. She was hardly a threat.

"Hey," she said gently, not wanting to startle her. "How are you feeling?"

Nat twisted her head to the side so abruptly it made Riley take a step back. "Who are you?"

"I'm Riley Tanner. This is my daughter, Brooke." She coaxed her daughter forward so Nat could see her, praying their bond would help break through the injured woman's confusion. "You were staying with us when you got hurt."

"I-I don't remember." Nat's face crumpled. "They tell me I'm in Oregon. Do you live in Oregon?"

"We do. You've only been with us for a few days, which is probably why you don't remember. You were helping us."

"Helping you? With what?" Nat's face was unnervingly blank, but her eyes were not. They were as sharp as ever, which gave Riley hope. Without the woman's wits, and her expertise, they were sunk—that was, if she had the nerve to return to the "monster house" at all, which Riley wasn't sure she did.

Checking over her shoulder to make sure the nurse wasn't hovering nearby, Riley decided to be honest. Lying wouldn't help Nat's memory return any faster. If anything, it would confuse her more. "With our Sasquatch problem."

Nat's jaw hardened. "The creatures. They *are* real."

Riley was so relieved she could have collapsed into the nearest chair. "Yes. We've seen it. Both of us have seen it."

For the first time, Nat appeared to notice Brooke. Her expression softened. "Hello, Brooke."

Brooke looked shy all of a sudden. She came forward to touch Nat's hand. "Hi."

"Are you okay? They didn't hurt you, did they?"

Riley didn't miss the threatening note in the woman's voice, and she was glad she wasn't the only one who cared that much about protecting Brooke. With Jason gone so often, she'd felt unnervingly vulnerable.

"No," Brooke said. "You were the one who got hurt. Does your head ache?"

The corners of Nat's mouth trembled. "A little. But I'll be okay. I've survived worse." She looked up at Riley. "What happened?"

"I don't really know. We didn't see it. One minute, you rushed outside to confront the creature, and the next, you were on the ground."

"That's not true, Mom. We saw it hit Nat, remember? It swung its arm like this…" Brooke made a massive swiping gesture, baring her teeth, "…and got Nat right across the head."

She *didn't* remember. Had she turned away during that crucial moment, or blocked it out?

"The doctor says my skull was cracked. This creature is playing for keeps." Nat tried to smile again, and Riley wished she knew whether or not it was appropriate to hug her. Since they'd met, Nat had kept her at a distance, with a wall between them that was impossible to penetrate. She wasn't sure if that was Nat's personality, or her attempt to maintain professionalism between them. Or perhaps Riley wasn't her cup of tea. It was impossible to tell.

"It's healing well, though. Now that you're conscious, you should be able to go home soon." Riley hoped she sounded more optimistic than she felt. The nurse had said the fracture was healing, but nothing about releasing Nat. She prayed the woman's insurance coverage was up to snuff. If not, maybe Jason could help. That was one of the few benefits of his job.

"Home?" Nat raised an eyebrow, and then winced as if it pained her. "You're done with me, then?"

"*Mom*," Brooke said through clenched teeth, digging her nails into Riley's palm, but Riley ignored her. If there were ever a time to put Nat's needs above theirs, it was now.

"We can't ask you to come back, not after what you've been through. You're seriously injured. Who knows how long it will take you to recover? We can't risk anything else happening to you."

"A wounded general may step away from the front lines, but there's nothing wrong with his mind," Nat muttered.

"What are you saying? If I were in your shoes, I'd never want to see that house again." Riley fought against her rising hopes. If she were a decent person, if she cared about her fellow (wo)man at all, she should discourage this. What if the creature had a hate-on for Nat now? What if it ripped her apart the first time it saw her again? "I'm not sure *I* do. We've decided to stay in town until Jason returns, get a bit of a breather." Sparing her some of the gory details, she quickly filled Nat in on the destroyed door and the smelly calling card.

"It's marking its territory. It's claiming your house as his," Nat said. "Are you going to stand for that?"

"If it means we can move on with our lives, then yes. No house is worth risking our lives." Riley hugged her daughter close again, forever reminded by her presence that some things were more important than money—or pending financial ruin.

"That's where we're different. I've faced death too many times to count and lived to tell." Nat focused on Riley, her expression stern and unwavering. No wonder she got along so well with Brooke—their stubbornness was a solid match. "Besides, I've got a score to settle."

CHAPTER ELEVEN

"What in the living Christ is this?" Anxious from the lack of response from his wife and daughter, Jason Tanner jumped down from his rig and hit the ground running at the sight of several unfamiliar trucks. A group of strangers were clustered on his front porch. Strangers with tools.

"Excuse me," he said, raising his voice to be heard over a drill. The man crouched by his front door squinted up at him, while the others paid him a cursory glance at best before resuming their work. "Would you mind telling me who you are?"

"Depends," said the man with the drill. He had a shock of bright white hair and startling blue eyes. It was a combination Riley had always found "striking," and jealously, Jason wondered if that's why the man was there. But that was ridiculous. The man was too old to be his wife's lover, and even if she'd acquired a grandfather fetish while he'd been on the road, why would he be replacing their door? "Who are you?"

With his pulse pounding in his temples, Jason felt his worry and fear convert to rage. These fuckers were trespassing on *his* property, and they were demanding *his* name? "I'm Jason Tanner," he said, making himself unclench his fists. Best not to christen his homecoming with striking a man old enough to be his father. "I own this place. That's my house you're working on."

If he'd expected deference, or some meager level of respect, he was disappointed. The man merely tipped his head before returning to his work on the door. "Afternoon. Always good to put a face to the name that'll be on my check."

"Do you mind telling me what you're doing here? Why are you replacing that door? What was wrong with the old one?"

For the first time since he'd arrived, he appeared to capture everyone's attention. The four men stopped working long enough to exchange a *look*. It reminded Jason of a phrase he'd found amusing ever since he'd learned it in high school

English: *pregnant with meaning.* If anyone was capable of looks that were pregnant with meaning, it was these dudes.

The older man, obviously the designated spokesperson for the group, cleared his throat. "The other one was torn clean off its hinges. Your wife wants something stronger. She wants steel."

"Steel?" Dollar signs temporarily obstructed Jason's vision. He noticed the industrial appearance of the new door. It was steel, all right. Steel, and ugly as fuck. What on earth was Riley thinking? Was this some crazy idea that woman from California had put in her head?

"I see it don't match the look of your house, and I'm sorry about that. I offered to order something special in, have something customized, but your wife said this was an emergency." The older man clicked his tongue. "It's too late to change it now. If you have a problem with it, I suggest you talk to her."

He'd love to talk to her, if he could get a response. *Dammit, Riley, where are you?* But tempering his frustration was the knowledge that this wasn't like his wife. Riley was a responsible person, much more responsible than he was. Even if this seemed like a rash decision, he could be assured it wasn't. It wasn't like her not to answer her phone, either, but if she was ordering new doors, she was alive, at least.

"Can you tell me what happened? You said the old door was torn off its hinges. I get that—but how?"

This time a different man spoke. He was thin and wiry, with a resemblance to a hungry cat. "Looks to me an animal did it. There was a great load of scat we had to clean out of the way in order to start the job." He wrinkled his nose. "That's not what we do. We're not a cleaning crew. Guess your woman was in too big a hurry to get ready for us."

Jason didn't care for his tone. Riley wasn't "his woman" any more than Jason was her personal property. "Scat?"

Before the man could respond, Jason waved him off. "I know what it is. I just don't understand what animal could have done this."

The crew exchanged another look, and Jason had a feeling they didn't believe him for a second. "No?" the older man said, skepticism weighing down his words. "Perhaps you should ask your wife about that too."

* * *

As soon as Riley plugged in her phone, it rang. She didn't have to look to know who it was—Jason. *He must be frantic by now.* Sitting on the firm-but-passable bed in their new temporary home in the inn, she braced herself for her husband's wrath. He was a pretty mild-mannered guy, but she figured even mild-mannered guys had their limits. Mentally crossing her fingers, she prayed Rod hadn't contacted him directly about the bill. She was hoping to handle that in her own way, her own time.

"Hi, honey. How's life on the road?" she asked, striving for brightness but hating the syrupy tone of her voice. It sounded fake as saccharin. No way he would buy it.

He didn't. "What the hell is going on? Wait—before you answer that—where's Brooke? Is she okay? Are *you* okay?"

"We're fine. Sorry we've been out of commission. My phone ran out of juice."

"That's all right. I'm just glad to hear your voice. I've been going out of my mind here."

"I'm sorry, sweetie. I didn't notice my phone was dead until the hospital told me they couldn't get through." Riley realized what she'd said when it was too late to take it back. *Damn.*

"The hospital?" Jason's voice cracked, and he coughed. "Then something *is* wrong."

"It's not us; it's Nat. She—she had an accident. A bad one. She's still in the hospital. I haven't had a chance to talk to her about insurance, but she may need our help."

"Fine, fine. That's not a problem. Just tell me what happened before I lose my mind."

"Mom?"

Riley looked over at Brooke, who stood in front of her, twisting her fingers. "What is it, honey?"

"Can I have a shower?"

Lately her little girl had taken to showers, eschewing her usual bubble baths. Yet another sign of impending teenage-hood. "Don't you want to talk to your dad first?"

To her surprise, her daughter shook her head, her hair swinging in a wide curtain behind her. "Tell him I'll text him later."

That was strange. Daddy's little girl avoiding the number-one man in her life? Of course, the last forty-eight hours had been quite the ride. Perhaps Brooke needed some processing time too. "Okay." After the girl had disappeared into the bathroom, Riley murmured into the phone, "Your daughter says she'll text you later."

"I heard. Nothing makes a man feel more special than finding out his little girl can't be assed to talk to him." Thankfully, Jason sounded more bemused than hurt.

"She's not so little anymore, Jay. I'm seeing more and more signs of impending adolescence."

"As if we don't have enough problems. So what happened to Nat?"

"First night you left, it came back, pounding on the walls like it was determined to bust right through. Nat had insisted we do our usual movie thing, so we did, not like we could pay any attention to the film. She stayed in the kitchen by herself, and something must have set her off, because the next thing I knew, she was screaming for my gun and running outside like a woman possessed."

"You mean like you did last time?"

"Ha, ha. This was different. She ran around the side of the house and challenged the thing, dared it to show itself. Well…it accepted the challenge."

"It attacked her?" A wariness had crept into Jason's voice. Riley figured it was one thing to humor your family's claims about a strange creature, and another when that figment of imagination actually started hurting people.

"Knocked her to the ground, cracked her skull. She's been in a coma. Seems to be recovering now, though. She actually wants to come back to the house when she's released." *Though I'm not sure I do.*

"Jesus. Can she sue us?"

"Jason Aaron Tanner. Is that really the first question that came to mind when you heard our guest is in the hospital with a big crack running through her skull? Why is money always the first thing with you?"

"Geez, I don't know, Riley. Maybe it's the fact we don't have enough of it? That one misstep could send us into bankruptcy?"

His response chastened her. Besides, he hadn't hired Nat, hadn't seen what happened to her. He didn't have the same responsibility or attachment to her. "You're right. I'm sorry."

"Did it come in after you?"

"What?" Riley asked, confused.

"It—the creature. Did it come into the house after you?"

"No. Thank God. Why do you ask?" It seemed an odd question.

"I've been to the house. I met your team of merry gentlemen outfitting the place like Fort Knox."

"They're there already?" Just the knowledge that the door would be repaired, the house sealed shut by the time they returned, made her feel better. She hadn't entirely trusted Rod to take care of it. "Good."

"Yes, they're there. Friendly bunch." The sarcasm dripped from his words like ice water. "Practically demanded my identification before they would talk to me."

"I haven't met them. I called Rod, told him to arrange it. Figured it was the least he could do."

Jason snorted. "Hopefully he won't add his services to the bill as well. I understand how you feel honey, but do you think it's necessary? By the look of it, that door is better suited to a fallout shelter."

She breathed deeply through her nose, telling herself that lashing out at her husband was not the answer. "Did you happen to see the old one?"

"I got a glimpse of it, yeah."

His flippant tone made her angrier. "Thankfully, me and your daughter were at the hospital with Nat when that thing ripped it apart like cheap clingfilm, but what if we hadn't been? What if we'd been home?" Before Jason could respond, the other shoe dropped. The piece of the puzzle that hadn't fit slipped into place. "Wait, you're *here*? You're home?"

"Of course I'm home. With everything that's been going on, I flipped when I couldn't reach you. Cut the job short and came straight back."

Riley buried her head in her hands. Yet another expense they couldn't afford. Why, oh why, hadn't she charged her damn phone? There was no reason for Jason to be here, not when they could await his return at the inn. For the moment, the crisis had passed. "What a mess. I'm so sorry."

His voice softened. "Hey, forget about it. None of this is your fault. We'll find a way to pay for it, even if I have to work overtime for the rest of my natural life. The important thing is that you and Brooke are okay."

"And Nat." Riley sniffed, wiping her eyes. Her husband's sympathy had reawakened all the feelings she'd been holding at bay—the terror, the worry, the anger. She'd been chased out of her home by a creature no one believed existed. No one except for Brooke. And Nat. And an outspoken girl who'd set up camp in the local library.

"Yes, and Nat. So where are you now?"

"We're at the Longview Inn." She could hear his mental calculator working overtime. "We couldn't bear to go back to the house yet. Don't worry. I got some design work last week, and I have room on my Visa. I'll cover it."

"But what about tomorrow? And the day after that? Will you feel comfortable there again? How can I possibly leave you there alone with Brooke after everything that's happened?"

She'd been wondering the same thing, but trying not to think about it, because she didn't have the answer yet. *"Take it one step at a time,"* her grandmother used to say whenever something problematic came up, and it seemed like as good advice as any in this situation. "We won't be alone," she said, simply because she couldn't think of anything else to say. "We'll have Nat."

"No offense, honey, but that didn't help you much last time."

"This will be different. We're going to use her brains, not her...shooting arm."

"If you don't mind, I'd like to come up with something a little more forceful than that. Show this creature exactly who's boss."

It already knows who's boss. That's the problem. "Fine."

"Oh no, she's 'fine-ing' me. That's the kiss of death right there. Would it make it up to you if I took my two best girls out to dinner?"

"What, to McDonald's?" She couldn't resist teasing, though she knew she shouldn't. To Jason, their financial situation was no laughing matter.

"No, somewhere nice. Might as well. We're in this deep already. What's another inch?"

"As long as it's not too nice. We forgot to pack our ball gowns."

"Fair enough. Now that you mention it, my tux *is* at the cleaner's. Family-friendly it is."

"Family-friendly works. We *are* a family, after all."

"And we're mostly friendly."

"I love you, Jay. I'm glad you're home."

He hooted. "Mission accomplished! She likes me again."

"I always liked you. You know that. I wouldn't put up with your ugly mug otherwise."

"True. It is one mighty big cross to bear. I'm out by the house, so I'll see you in about half an hour."

"Okay." She hesitated, wondering how best to word her next request. Her husband had driven through the night, traveling umpteen miles to get there. He probably wasn't going to take kindly to her plan. Still, best to prepare him now. "Jay?"

"Yeah?"

"You still packed?"

"Yep. Why? You fancy having a love-in at the Longview Inn?"

"Not exactly. I was thinking of going on a little road trip before we return to the house."

"Where to?"

Squeezing her eyes shut, she said the words before she could think better of it. "Phoenix."

The explosion was immediate. "Phoenix? As in, Arizona? Jesus Christ, Riley. That's not a 'little' road trip. That's a sixteen-hour drive, thirty-two hours round trip."

"Do you think there's any possibility of picking up some work along the way? Someone must need something in Nevada."

Jason sucked in a breath. "I guess it's possible. But Christ, that means I'm driving the whole time again. I just got back. It's dangerous to drive too much without a break, Ry."

"I know, but I promise to be *really* entertaining. I'll keep you awake." She realized as soon as she'd said it that her words sounded seductive, though she hadn't meant them that way.

Her husband's voice lowered. "That could be dangerous too."

"Not like *that*. We'll have Brooke with us, remember? Please, Jason. I wouldn't ask if it weren't important. It could be a matter of life or death."

"Okay, I'll bite. What on earth is in Phoenix, Arizona?"

"The Riordans."

"The roy-or-*who*?"

"The Riordans. The ones who sold us the house at such a sweet price because they were afraid of a few owls and bears." She couldn't keep the bitterness from creeping into her voice.

"Oh, right. *Them.* Couldn't we give them a call? It would be a lot cheaper. Not to mention a lot faster."

"I'm going to make some calls to find them, but I think we'll have better luck getting them to talk if we're on their doorstep. Especially when they see there's a child involved."

"You're probably right, honey, but what makes you think talking to them is going to help? If they had any answers, they'd have stayed in the house, right? They must have taken quite a hit to sell it at that price."

"Maybe. I don't know. I can't explain it, but this is one of those times when you're going to have to trust your wife's intuition. There's something not right about this entire situation. You should have heard Rod today—he acted like I was the FBI, the CIA, and the KGB rolled into one." She paused, hoping for a word of encouragement, but Jason remained silent. At least he wasn't arguing, or worse, mocking her. "These people know something. I don't know what it is, and I'm not sure it's going to help us. But I'm determined to find out."

CHAPTER TWELVE

Franklin Riordan turned to the sports section of his newspaper with a self-satisfied sigh. When was the last time they'd enjoyed such a relaxing weekend? When had he last felt so at peace?

"Franklin?"

Elizabeth peered through the curtains, scrutinizing whatever was going on across the street. Ordinarily, *nothing* was going on. His wife insisted upon acting like they were fugitives, as if John Walsh and his crew would descend on them at any moment, dragging them to prison. He figured her paranoia would diminish with time. Until then, he'd developed two coping mechanisms: ignore her or humor her.

"Yes, dear?" He hoped his voice didn't sound as world-weary as he felt. Why couldn't she let it go? They were safe now, weren't they?

"That couple is back."

"So? They're probably selling something."

"I don't think so." Elizabeth risked another peek and jerked back from the window as if she'd been burned. "The neighbors are pointing at our house."

He shrugged. "Maybe they think we'll be interested in buying what they're selling. Who knows?"

"No," she said, her voice wavering. "They're looking for us. I can feel it. I knew they would find us eventually. It was only a matter of time."

Franklin made a note to donate his wife's book collection to Goodwill the next time she left the house. All that reading about Bigfoot and Sasquatches and Yetis hadn't been helping her paranoia. She claimed it made her feel better, knowing they weren't alone, but he had no desire to become one of the crazies babbling about giant humanoid creatures covered in hair. They were right up there with the nutjobs who claimed to have been abducted by aliens.

"Now, why would anyone be looking for us?" he asked, keeping his tone mild, as if it were the most ludicrous thing in the world and hardly worth considering.

Elizabeth tore the newspaper out of his hands, crumpling it before tossing it across the room.

"Hey!"

"You know damn well why they'd be looking for us, Frank. What we did was wrong." She didn't sound scared now—she sounded furious, as if she'd kill him as soon as look at him. Not for the first time, Franklin felt a little afraid of his wife.

"How was it wrong?" Feeling at a loss without his paper, he snatched the rubber stress ball from the end table and began to squeeze. It was the third one he'd gone through since the move. Damn things weren't made as well they used to be, but then again, nothing was. "We sold a house, nothing more. People are allowed to sell their homes, Beth."

"Don't you talk to me like I'm a child. You know *exactly* what I mean." Her teeth clenched, she lunged toward him, leaving him no room to escape. Her breath was foul, smelling of stale coffee, and he cringed. "We were deceptive. That has to be illegal. Everyone in that godforsaken damn town knows exactly why we left, including Rod Silver."

"How were we deceptive? It's not like the place has a cracked foundation or leaky pipes. You told Rod about the 'wildlife,' and like you said, everyone knows what that means. The new owners were probably overjoyed to get that place for a song, and we were happy to get the hell out of there. So what's the problem?"

Before she could answer, someone pounded on the door. Her rage gone, Elizabeth gasped and ducked behind his chair.

"They've found us. I told you they would."

Ordinarily, Franklin wouldn't have bothered opening the door, but he thought it was worthwhile this time, if only to prove to Elizabeth that her fears were all in her head. If he ended up having to shoo away a family of Jehovah's Witnesses, or buy a few boxes of Girl Scout cookies, it was worth it.

As he rose from the recliner, Elizabeth's hand snaked around the side of the chair and clung to his arm. "Don't answer it. It's *them*."

Who were *they*, anyhow? The police? Rod Silver? The creatures themselves? He'd never seen the point in asking. "It's no one, darling, and I'll prove it to you."

He opened the door as the man raised his fist to pound on it again. Whoever these people were, they were too casually dressed to be Jehovah's Witnesses. The man sported a plaid, flannel jacket over a dirty white Henley and jeans that had been worn to threads. A reddish cap, fading to pink and also dirty, was pulled low over his brow, while a dark beard concealed the rest of his face. Seeing this strange, dust-coated man at his door, Franklin thought his wife might have had a point. But the guy wasn't alone—he had a woman and a young girl with him, and the females looked a hell of a lot less sinister.

"Yes? Can I help you?" Franklin said, praying they weren't there to shove their way in and rob them. The Riordans didn't have much left to steal.

"Mr. Riordan?" the woman asked. She was soft-spoken and attractive, with a breathy, Marilyn Monroe-quality to her voice, but as she met his eyes, he was shocked to see hatred reflected back at him. *What's going on? Who are these people?*

He drew himself up to his full height, which wasn't much compared to the man at his door. "Who wants to know?"

"Mr. Riordan, we've driven from Oregon to talk to you."

At the mention of the state that had once been home, he felt his angina act up, clutching his heart in a vise and squeezing. He grabbed the door frame for support. "Oregon? I-I'm afraid I don't understand. Who *are* you people?"

The man spoke for the first time, his voice a lot kinder than his appearance would suggest. "We're the people who bought your house."

"We've been expecting you," Elizabeth said from behind him, sounding more confident than she had since their nightmare began. "Let them in, Frank. Let's get this over with."

Franklin hesitated. How could they know these people were who they claimed to be? But there was something in their faces, especially the young girl's and the woman's—the dark circles, the unnaturally pale complexions, that haunted look. Elizabeth had looked the same way before they moved. He stepped aside, allowing them into the house, well aware the neighbors were watching. *Christly busybodies.* But privacy came with a high price, as they'd discovered. Though irritating, it was best to have other people keeping an eye on you.

"Can I get you something to drink?"

Franklin gaped at his wife as she whirled into hostess mode, as if these three strangers were dear friends dropping by for a visit. "Tea, coffee? I'm afraid I don't have any soda, but we have some orange juice in the fridge. Or I can make iced tea."

"Coffee would be wonderful, if you don't mind," the man said, glancing at the woman. "For both of us."

"What would you like, dear?" Elizabeth, who'd always longed for children but couldn't have them, was in her element with any child. "I have some flavored sparkling water too, now that I think of it."

"That would be nice, thank you," the girl mumbled, staring at her feet. There was an oddly robotic quality to her voice. She'd experienced some sort of trauma, and Franklin hoped it had nothing to do with the house—with *it.* They'd been clear with Rod from the start, had specifically insisted that whomever he sold the house to couldn't have children. The Riordans weren't *monsters,* after all.

Franklin coughed. "Oregon. That's a long way."

"Not to me. I'm a long-haul trucker," the man said. "Please forgive my appearance; I just finished work before heading here."

"We can't rescind the sale, if that's what you're after." Franklin felt it was best to get it out right up front. "We lost our shirt as it is."

"Frank…" Elizabeth said, giving their uninvited guests an embarrassed smile to apologize for her bumbling husband and his lack of social graces.

"To be quite honest with you, I'm not sure why we're here. This was my wife's idea." The man took his wife's hand and she gave him a semblance of a smile, the first one Franklin had seen since they'd arrived.

"Why don't we all sit down?" Elizabeth gestured to the kitchen table. She pulled over the small chair from the writing desk for the child. "My name is Elizabeth Riordan, but you can call me Beth. This is my husband Franklin, but if you've come this far, I suspect you already know that."

"It wasn't easy to find you," the man said. "My wife had to play detective. The real estate agent wouldn't tell us anything."

"Well, he wouldn't." Franklin was pleased. He'd never trusted that man Rod. Something about him had always struck Frank as slimy. But at least he'd kept his word about protecting their privacy, as far as it went. "That was part of the agreement."

"I'm Riley Tanner," the woman said, offering her hand to Elizabeth. "This is my daughter, Brooke, and my husband, Jason."

"I'd love to say I'm pleased to meet you, but the truth is, I've been dreading this," his wife said in an uncharacteristic fit of brutal honesty. "I had a feeling you'd come."

"That's good then, right?" Jason Tanner removed his cap, running his hands through dark, curly hair. "No need to beat around the bush, or pretend we're talking about owls and bears."

Franklin felt his eyebrows rise. "Owls and bears? Is that what he told you?"

The man nodded, collapsing into a chair as if he were too exhausted to hold himself upright any longer. "Yessir. You were city people, and the local wildlife got to be too much for you."

Franklin smirked. "Local wildlife, indeed. Beth grew up in the country, and while I wouldn't exactly consider my place of birth rural, it was hardly the big city." He couldn't be too hard on Rod, though. The man had to create *some* explanation for why they'd flown the coop, so to speak.

Elizabeth coaxed Riley and Brooke into chairs, bringing over the coffee carafe with some cream and sugar. "You can't blame him, Franklin," she said, as if reading his mind. Shifting her attention to their visitors, she explained, "We told him he could come up with any story he liked. I suppose he did his best."

Seeing he wasn't about to be served, Franklin got his own coffee cup, along with a glass of sparkling mixed-berry flavored water for the girl. "He never should have sold the house to you, though. We specifically said no children." Realizing how that sounded, he gave the girl what he hoped was a sympathetic smile. "We didn't think it was a safe place for young people."

"It's not a safe place for older ones, either," Jason said, stirring sugar into his cup. "We now have a friend in the hospital, recovering from a fractured skull."

Elizabeth dropped a spoon on the floor, the resulting clatter making all three Tanners flinch. "Oh no—they were never violent with us, *never*. Is your friend going to be all right?"

"We hope so," Riley said. "She's disoriented, but she's strong. Isn't she, Brooke?"

The girl nodded without looking up. She appeared to be transfixed by the bubbles in her drink.

"A woman? Oh, no—I'm so sorry. How did this happen?" Elizabeth asked.

"It attacked her, that's what happened. She was defending my family when it knocked her off her feet and cracked her skull." Jason narrowed his eyes at her. "I couldn't help but notice you said 'they.' Am I to take it there's more than one?"

"Oh yes, there's a family. At least, we thought they were a family, but I guess there's no way to tell for sure. We never saw any little ones."

"Thank Christ for that," Jason said. "Did you tell Rod the truth about why you wanted to sell?"

Franklin shook his head. "There was no need. Everyone in Longview knows about that place. They call it the—"

"Monster House. We know that...*now*," Riley said. "But why did you buy it, if you knew?"

"Same reason you did, I suspect. The owners were selling at a cut-rate price, and we both liked the idea of having some privacy. We didn't pay much attention to the stories. That fellow Rod made it sound like the sort of thing children tell each other around the campfire. We didn't believe it was real."

"Neither did I," Jason admitted. "But now we have a friend in the hospital and a ruined front door. I can't take a job without worrying about what I'm going to find when I get back, and for Brooke and Riley—well, it's been a nightmare."

Elizabeth met Franklin's eyes, the shock plain on her face. "This is quite disturbing. They frightened us, yes, but they were never violent, never destructive. I can't understand why they're reacting this way to you."

"Something about Nat—our friend—seemed to set them off, but they've always been aggressive, pounding on our house like they want to break through the wall. They've broken the kitchen window, and the other night they tore the front door off its hinges." Riley took a sip of her coffee, her hands trembling. "They only come around when Jason is out of town—it's as if they know when he leaves. And every time, it gets worse. I'm afraid of what will happen next."

"Oh, they're smart buggers, no doubt about it," Franklin said, wishing his wife made better coffee. The current brew was tarlike, with a distinctive charred flavor. He had no idea how their visitors were choking it down. "They're not like ordinary animals. They *watch*."

"But why?" Riley said, her voice breaking. "What do they *want*?"

Elizabeth laid her hand over the woman's. "I've always thought they were curious. I will admit it scared the bejesus out of me when I'd catch them staring in the kitchen window, or wandering around the outside of the house, but they were never violent."

"Then why did you move?" Jason asked. "That doesn't sound too bad to me. Certainly not worth losing your shirt over."

"It got to be too much," Franklin said. "At first, we barely caught a glimpse of them, but then they got bolder. Got so they were always peering in our windows or lurking around the house. Beth was a nervous wreck. We could hear them at night, rustling around. Couldn't get a lick of sleep."

Elizabeth raised an eyebrow. "*I* was a nervous wreck? That's hardly fair, Frank."

"Okay, okay, so we both were. I don't mind admitting it—those things unnerved me. They're unnatural. I was glad to leave that place behind." He reached for his coffee, but then thought better of it. It was almost four o'clock. How much grief would Beth give him if he grabbed a beer?

Jason exchanged a look with Riley. "I wish that was all that was happening to us. We could probably live with that. But with the way things are going, we don't want to go back to the house. And I don't feel comfortable leaving my girls there alone."

"It's gotten so we're afraid to go outside," Riley added. "Or to let Brooke go outside. We're prisoners in our own home, and I'm terrified."

"Let's cut to the chase. What do you expect from us?" Franklin hadn't moved that far away to relive the whole damn thing again. "We sold the house at a low price, in good faith. We had no way of knowing those things would turn against you, or even who you were."

Anger flashed across the man's face, and he opened his mouth to respond, but Riley put a hand over his. "I don't really know. I guess we hoped you'd have answers of some kind, some idea of why they've become so aggressive and violent," she said. "But if they weren't this way with you..."

"They weren't. To be honest, miss, it would be for the best if you had Animal Control or the police or whoever takes care of this kind of situation come out there and shoot the damn things."

"Franklin!" Beth tipped her head at the child, who hadn't looked up from her drink. Or tasted it, from what she could see.

"Sorry. But that would be my best advice. Hell, if those things had terrorized *my* wife, I would have put a bullet in their heads myself."

"Um...so far, we haven't had much luck in the gun department," Jason said. "I'm not sure that's the best solution."

"Nat—our friend—had my shotgun when she was injured," Riley added.

"It seems they aren't as aggressive when you're around," Franklin said to Jason. "Is that right?"

"I haven't seen them. They only bother Riley and Brooke when I'm on the road."

"Well, there you have it. Defend your home, and your family. Shoot them."

"Franklin, I don't think that's a good idea," Beth said.

"Why the hell not?"

SHADOW OF THE SASQUATCH

"What if that makes them more aggressive? We have no idea how many there are."

"Then firebomb the woods. Get rid of them all." Franklin scowled. "If their hiding places are burned to the ground, they'll have no place to hide, will they? *Then* you can kill them."

"And what about the birds and other creatures who depend on that forest?" Riley said, her eyes watering. "No, I don't like that idea at all. We can't kill them."

Franklin shrugged. "Suit yourself. Sell the house then, I guess."

"And have another family go through this?" Jason asked. "It doesn't seem right."

"Maybe it won't be so bad for the next ones. It wasn't for us."

"We can't take that chance. Besides, we can't afford to move at the moment." The man's cheeks darkened to a brick red. "Our...financial situation isn't the greatest."

"Oh, you poor dears. I wish there was something we could do, something we could tell you," Beth said. She shot Franklin that beseeching glance that usually turned him to putty, but what did she expect *him* to do? He'd already given the strangers his best advice. "Maybe we should have stayed. We could go back..."

"Are you out of your mind, Beth? Do you remember what this place cost?" Franklin rose from the table, determined to get a beer whether she liked it or not. "We're not going anywhere. I don't know about you, but I could use a drink." He looked at Jason. "Would you like a beer?"

An expression of wistfulness crossed the man's face, but he shook his head. "I'd love one, but I better not. I've got a long drive ahead of me."

"I'd like one, please," Riley said, moving her half-full coffee cup slightly to the side.

Franklin nodded at her, surprised. He didn't often meet women who liked beer. Wine, or one of those damn-awful coolers that tasted like rotten fruit, sure. But never beer. "I don't have any of that fancy craft, pumpkin-flavored stuff. Just plain old Bud."

The woman looked bemused. "A Bud would be fine. Thank you."

"Glass?"

"In the can is great. Please don't dirty another dish on my account."

A woman after his own heart. Franklin retrieved the two beers from the fridge, ignoring the disapproving look his wife was surely sending in his direction. If discussing those *things* that had made their lives a living hell wasn't cause for a drink, he didn't know what was. "Like I said, I'm not sure what you want from us. We're happy to meet you, to jaw about our experiences at the house. But I'm not seeing how this helps you."

"Do you have any history on the house?" Riley asked. "Do you know who built it, or when people first started having problems there?"

"I tried to find out that very thing. I even went to the Town Hall and searched their archives," Elizabeth said, "but there was nothing. It's like some big secret that everyone knows about but that no one wants to discuss."

"That sounds a bit dramatic. Why would the town have records about an ordinary house?" Franklin said. "If there's nothing to say, there's nothing to say."

Elizabeth made a face. "It's hardly an ordinary house, Frank."

"Your wife is right. I know exactly what she's talking about. I went to the library before coming here, and the woman working there completely stonewalled me. Only some strange girl hanging out there had the guts to tell me the truth," Riley said. "She was the one who gave me your last name."

Elizabeth smiled. "That sounds like Clara. She's an interesting girl. Gives the place a bit of color."

"That's one word for it," Franklin muttered.

"Now, be nice. There's nothing wrong with being different." His wife made a disapproving sound under her breath.

"Calling that girl different is like saying the ocean is a little damp." He drained the rest of his beer, crushing the can just enough to hear that satisfying metallic crinkle. "I'm not surprised she was the one who told you. She never could keep her mouth shut."

"Well, it appears as if this is what my dad used to call a fool's errand," Jason said, pushing back from the table. "I'm sorry to have wasted your time, but we won't take up any more of it."

Before Franklin could relish this awkward experience coming to an end, his wife intervened. "Don't be ridiculous. You can't drive through the night again. It isn't safe."

Jason glanced at his wife. "We can't afford a hotel. If I get too tired, there's a bed in the back of the truck."

"Absolutely not. I won't hear of it. You'll stay with us tonight." Elizabeth's words tumbled over one another, as if she believed not giving them an opportunity to speak would convince them. "Frank will put some steaks and a few potatoes on the grill, and I'll make sure the sheets are fresh in the guestroom. It's a nice room, and there's space for an air mattress for your daughter."

This time it was her turn to ignore a withering look, but Franklin knew it was hopeless anyway. Once Beth got her mind made up about something, there was no stopping her.

"That's really kind." The man rubbed his forehead, looking at his wife. "Incredibly kind, but why would you want to do that? We're strangers, more or less."

"Not anymore, you're not. You folks came here for answers, and I think that, together, we can come up with something. Anything, as long as it gives your daughter a bit of peace." Elizabeth looked pointedly at Brooke, who was sitting slumped over in her chair, and Franklin saw the conflicting emotions on his wife's face. Seeing a child in peril was breaking her heart.

"If you're sure…" Riley said. "I *was* worried about Jason driving back again so soon. He always pushes too hard."

"I'm not only sure; I insist. We'll have a nice dinner, and then we'll decide what to do about your unwelcome guests. We got you into this, unintended or not." Elizabeth's lips hardened into that firm line Franklin knew so well. "It's our responsibility to help get you out."

CHAPTER THIRTEEN

When he was blissfully silent, which admittedly wasn't often, Nat could feel his disapproval. It oozed from his pores, infecting her space and keeping her from sleeping.

When his unspoken dissatisfaction didn't provoke a reaction, the sighing and huffing started. Nat closed her eyes and turned over in an attempt to shut him out. Now that she wasn't as violent and disoriented, the restraints had been removed, allowing her a little more freedom, not that her backless gown encouraged strolls.

He exhaled loudly, that timeless sound of extreme disappointment.

That was *it*. She'd had it.

"Don't you have something better to do?"

"Not at the present time, no."

"What exactly is your problem with me, anyway? Why won't you leave me alone?" Her voice broke on the last word, and she hated herself for it. He'd already seen her at her weakest.

"How can you lie there, rotting? Those *things* are out there. A young girl is in danger."

"Um, it's called a cracked skull, remember?" Nat pointed at her bandaged head, falling short of tapping it. She was afraid to touch it. "I'm lucky to be alive."

"Yes, you *are*. I wish you'd start acting like it."

"What do you expect me to do, Steven? They're not here right now—they went to Phoenix to hunt down the previous owners of the house. The best thing for me to do is to use this time to heal. Which I can't do if you keep badgering me."

He rolled his eyes. "At least you can't drink. That thing did you a favor when it dropped you on the head."

"Fuck you."

"Excuse me? What did you just say?" The woman in the next bed, deathly ill from diabetes but still looking like she could kick some serious ass, propped herself up on her elbows.

"Sorry," Nat said. "Talking to myself."

"Can you talk to yo'self a little quieter? I'm trying to watch the shows."

"Sure. Sorry." She collapsed back against her pillows in relief when the woman returned her attention to the T.V. If she didn't want to get moved to the psychiatric ward, she'd have to be more careful. The other woman couldn't see Steven, so what did that mean? Was he a ghost? A hallucination? A figment of her imagination? Her conscience? Surely to Christ she would have chosen a more amenable imaginary friend.

"You need to get out of here, Nat. You're wasting time."

She folded her arms across her chest. *I will. When I'm better.*

"Haven't you heard the expression, 'There's never a perfect time'?"

I don't think the person who said that was referring to patients recovering from skull fractures. This is the perfect time for me to rest, which you are keeping me from doing. Please go haunt someone else.

"Like who? Igor?" Steven made that sly snickering sound she'd come to loathe. "He's more pathetic than you are."

The insult against the man who'd become one of her dearest friends—okay, her only friend—made her seethe. *At least he survived. Which is more than I can say for you.*

He feigned a pained expression, but the smirk remained. "Low blow, Nat—low blow."

Will you please get out of here and let me sleep? I didn't think it was possible, but you're more annoying in death than you were in life.

"Tell you what—I'll make you a deal. I'll let you sleep alllll day long if you promise to get the hell out of here this evening. After dinner, when Princess Gangrene begins her much-needed beauty sleep, you bust out."

Bust out? Are you crazy? My head was cracked. There's no way it's healed yet.

"Hey, at least you have one. Do we have a deal, or not?"

Against her better judgment, Nat considered it. Risking her life would be worth it if it meant getting rid of him for a while. And she was damn tired of hospital food, not to mention lying in a bed all day, doing nothing. Come to think of it, a drink would be nice. Her mouth watered.

"Nope, none of that. Haven't you done enough damage to yourself? I need you clean for this."

Clean for what? What do you want from me, anyway?

"Really, Nat. Haven't you been listening? For our revenge, of course."

She had to admit he was pretty smart for a ghost, if that was what he was. She preferred to think he was some artifact produced by her own twisted mind, punishment for those interesting drugs she'd overindulged in back in the '90s.

After dinner—a lovely feast consisting of a single, overcooked pork chop with a cloying mushroom sauce, a scoop of instant mashed potatoes, and some canned peas that had a decidedly grey hue—Nat's roommate was out, her head tipped back on the pillow, mouth open, snoring loud enough to wake the dead. Which she did.

"All right, time to go."

What about the nurses?

"They're serving the other floors. Plus, they have evening meds to prepare. There's no better time, Nat. C'mon, you're not insured. It's not like they're gonna care."

Good point. Nat eased herself to a sitting position, relieved that for once, there was no answering shriek of pain from her shattered skull. Was she doing this? Was she really this insane? Because only the truly insane escaped from hospitals that were trying to heal them, she was pretty sure.

"See? You're fine. Told ya." Steven's smirk was back in full force. If she hadn't been able to see it, she would have heard it in his voice.

I haven't stood up yet. It's a little early for I told you so.

Holding on to her IV stand, she tensed her muscles and pulled herself upright. She'd already had to do this every time she needed to use the bathroom, so she knew her legs still worked, thank God.

"You're going to need to get rid of that." The apparition nodded at the IV. "You can hardly escape with that thing attached to you."

But what if I need it? Nat realized with a start that she'd never bothered to ask what was in it. She'd had something dripping into her veins for over a week and had no idea what it was.

"Nah, it's a glucose mixture. You were undernourished when you got here. Imagine that? Our little experience in the Ural Mountains has certainly changed you."

Screw you.

Gingerly peeling back the adhesive that held the needle in place, she wondered if she was destroying any hope she had of recovery.

"C'mon, Nat, you're a big girl. Pull that thing out and let's get a move on. The longer you dawdle, the more chance there is that someone's going to notice you're missing."

And where am I supposed to go? Have you seen this ensemble? It's not exactly "blend in" material. Not to mention I'm recovering from a serious injury. What do you expect me to do, go for a jog until I figure out what the hell it is you want?

Her fingers paused before smoothing the adhesive over the needle again. *Come to think of it, why am I taking orders from a ghost in the first place? This is bullshit.*

She collapsed on her bed, turning on her side again, trying her best not to look at her roommate, whose mouth was wide open and appeared oddly toothless.

"Give me a little credit. I'm hardly a ghost."

That was a relief. The last thing she needed was to be haunted, least of all by him. *What are you, then?*

"Consider me the last remaining particles of your rapidly dwindling intelligence."

Great. That was so much better.

* * *

He never would have believed it possible, but they had a nice evening. Once the Tanners had some good, wholesome food in their stomachs—and he could grill a mean steak, if he said so himself—and a couple of beers apiece, they noticeably relaxed. The fellow, Jason, had a sharp sense of humor and made them all laugh a few times, and Franklin finally understood what they'd been missing by isolating themselves from the rest of the neighborhood.

The little one stayed quiet over dinner. He would have thought that was her way—some kids were naturally shy and reserved, no big deal—if it weren't for the way the mother continually fussed over her, asking if she wanted something else to eat or drink.

"I think she's tired," Riley said, as if she were apologizing. "It's been a long day—a long week, actually."

"A long month," Jason added.

"It's understandable. Do you want me to show you the guestroom, honey?" Beth asked, and looked delighted when the girl nodded, even though she hadn't smiled. Poor woman would have made such a good mother. It was enough to make him feel guilty that he'd nixed the idea of adoption. Franklin couldn't imagine loving a child that wasn't his own the same way he'd love a biological son or daughter. It wouldn't be fair to the kid, he'd told himself. But maybe he'd been wrong.

Since the room ended up being too cramped with the air mattress, they'd planned to let Jason and Riley stay in the guestroom, and give the girl the pullout couch in the basement. But Riley had said her daughter would be better off upstairs, where even at night, streetlights shone through the second-floor windows and it was never completely dark.

* * *

Her heart went out to this child, who seemed so alone, so trapped in whatever miserable movie persisted in replaying over and over in her head. Beth understood what that was like. She'd felt the same way after the first time she'd seen the creatures, as if she were living in a horror movie that would never end.

At least the guestroom was pretty, with its rose-patterned wallpaper and crocheted afghan. She hadn't had time to truly fix it up yet, and certainly hadn't been expecting visitors so soon, but it would do. No creatures would be peering in *these* windows, and she figured that was the most important thing.

"What do you think?" she asked, hoping for some kind of reaction from the girl. Brooke had been in a trance-like state since the Tanners had arrived in their home, and Riley had confided that she was concerned about the girl. Beth was too.

"It's nice," the girl said in a robotic voice. "Thank you."

Beth decided it was worth a shot. What did she have to lose? Franklin was entertaining the Tanners in the kitchen, and doing it well, by the sounds of it—she could hear their guests laughing, and it made her smile. Her husband had always been in his element when he had an opportunity to play host for people, even if he did drink a bit more beer than she would have liked. She'd known he was in a funk—not because of the lost money, but because they'd both been cooped up alone in this house for far too long, not that he would have admitted it. They hadn't gotten around to any of the neighbors yet—she'd been too afraid to, too afraid word would spread about where they were, and someone would find them. But now that the "someone" *had* found them, it might have been the best possible thing that could have happened. No more looking over their shoulders, no more dreading the arrival of the mail, and better yet, the Tanners were pleasant people. She liked them, though she found Riley a little too rough around the edges for her taste. Where she came from, women didn't drink beer from a can, especially not in front of their children. But Franklin liked having a young woman he could joke around and share beers with, and that was what was important. Beth knew she was a bit too "prim and proper" for her husband sometimes, a bit too precious, but she couldn't help it. That was the way she'd been raised. Riley was like the daughter they'd never had.

It was silly to think this way—they barely knew these people, and after tonight, they'd probably never see them or hear from them again. But there was no harm in it, and the only person who would be hurt by it in any way would be her. No one else needed to know, and if Riley was the daughter they'd never had, Brooke was their granddaughter. Beth had always known she'd have been the world's best grandmother. This was her chance to prove it.

Sitting down on the bed, she smoothed the afghan and patted the space next to her, wishing she had a teddy bear or other toy that would make the room more inviting to a child. "Will you sit with me for a minute?"

Brooke barely raised her head, but she obediently did what Beth asked, keeping a respectful distance.

"I can tell something's bothering you. Sometimes it helps to talk about it."

The child raised her shoulders and let them drop, staring at her hands, and for a moment, Beth thought it had been pointless. Oh, well. At least she'd tried. But then she heard the child mumble something, so quietly she couldn't make it out.

"What was that, dear? Are you worried about going back to the house? I can understand that, you know. I used to be so scared there during the night. I never knew who was peeping in at me through the windows." The second she said the words, Beth wished she could take them back. Talking about her own fears was hardly reassuring. She was the adult. She needed to be the brave one.

"I'm more worried about Nat," Brooke said, the first coherent sentence she'd spoken since she'd arrived. When she looked at Beth, Beth's heart ached to see the girl's face was streaked with tears. She handed her a tissue from the box near the bed.

"You care about Nat a lot, don't you?"

The girl nodded. "She's my only friend right now. I don't know anyone in Longview."

"Oh, well, it won't stay that way for long, not for a nice girl like you. Once school starts, you're going to make a gazillion friends."

"They won't be like Nat. Nat is special."

Eek. Despite her best efforts, she wasn't doing very well at this. She might have to rethink her "best grandmother in the world" delusions. "Of course she is. Would you like to tell me about her?"

Beth held her breath, waiting for the girl to say no, and tell her to buzz off, or whatever it was kids said these days. But this time, her grandmotherly instincts must have been right, for Brooke showed the most enthusiasm Beth had seen from her so far.

"She's the coolest person *ever*. She climbs trees like a monkey, and she isn't scared of anything. When those monsters were threatening us, she ran right up to them. She protected us."

She also wound up with a fractured skull. Maybe confronting the creatures wasn't the smartest idea, Beth thought, but of course she would never say those thoughts out loud. And, in this Nat's defense, some animals did respond well to intimidation. With these creatures, it was impossible to say what would work and what wouldn't. At least this woman had tried.

She hadn't run away, like they had.

"She sounds very brave," Beth said, and meant it.

"She is. She's the bravest person in the world." Brooke's voice faltered. "I'm scared she's going to die."

"Oh dear, I think she is going to be okay. People like Nat are very strong. She's not going to let those creatures get the better of her."

"She already did, once. She went to Russia and a bunch of people died. Her best friend too. She doesn't think I know, but I looked her up on the internet."

Beth felt out of her element. She didn't know anything about Russia, or how the creatures at her former home in Longview, Oregon could possibly be connected. But it didn't matter, because she thought she *did* know what to say this time. "But she survived, didn't she?"

"Yeah."

She could tell Beth was turning this over in her mind. "I bet she's going to survive this time too. Do you want to help her?"

Brooke looked up at her with those big brown eyes of hers, and it was all Beth could do not to melt. "How? What could I do?"

"We could send her healing vibes."

"How do you do that?"

"You close your eyes and picture the person you want to help, and then you send them every good thought you possibly can. With Nat, you want to imagine her well and healthy, leaving the hospital without a care in the world."

"Will this work?"

Beth thought for a moment about the best way to phrase it. She didn't want to mislead the child, or have Brooke believe they were going to perform a miracle. "I think positive thoughts always help. It certainly can't hurt. Do you want to try it?"

Brooke nodded, and Beth offered her hand. When the girl took it, Beth closed her eyes, peeking once to make sure Brooke had done the same. "Please send our love and light to

Nat," she said. "We send her our strength so she can get better."

"Please get better, Nat," the girl added. "We need you."

Listening outside the door, Riley smiled and walked away.

CHAPTER FOURTEEN

If Nat had been able to hear Brooke's praise, she would have either laughed or cried. She hardly felt like the bravest person in the world at the moment. Riley's daughter had no idea how scared Nat was most of the time.

As for the healing vibes, she certainly could have used them. Her head ached something awful.

It didn't seem wise to remove the bandages that were probably keeping her skull in one piece, but thankfully her roommate had an oversized hat that covered them, along with most of Nat's face. With the hat and the woman's shirt and overalls, which hung off her to the point of falling off, she resembled the world's strangest-looking farmer. She felt badly about stealing her roommate's clothes, but she couldn't find any of her own—they must have been destroyed in "the incident,"—and she could hardly be seen in public in the backless gown. She vowed to return them, freshly washed.

The key to getting away with stuff was appearing like you weren't doing anything wrong. That's what Andrew had always said. It was time to put his theory to the test.

She made it as far as the doorway without her head splitting apart. *Good.* She wasn't in the ICU anymore, which was a good thing—less hustle and bustle. Whether a ghost or an indication of her insanity, Steven was quiet now, and she wasn't sure if this was positive or negative. While he'd been driving her crazy (assuming that ship hadn't already sailed), at least he'd been company, someone to talk to, if only in her mind. And he certainly would have told her if she made a mistake.

Nat ducked back inside as a nurse hurried by, but the man didn't notice her. Another good sign. Taking a deep breath for courage and wishing she had a shot of something—*anything*—she left the room, trying to walk as casually as one could when their pants were in constant danger of falling down.

There's the elevator.

Steady now.

How many feet away? Ten? Twelve?

She could do it, assuming the pants held up and her skull stayed together.

It felt like the longest walk in the universe, especially on legs that were out of practice, and she nearly crumpled with relief when the elevator arrived empty.

Slipping into the elevator, she pressed P for Parkade, suspecting she was least likely to cause attention there.

Ding. The elevator stopped on the first floor, and the doors opened. *Shit.* Nat lowered her head and watched two feet get on. The feet were wearing sensible white sneakers, the kind nurses often wore. *Double shit.* She kept her head down, but could feel the uncomfortable sensation of eyes burning a hole into her. Finally, she risked a look. It wasn't like they were going to send her to prison for leaving a hospital. She was hardly doing anything illegal.

Except for stealing a woman's clothes and evading a really big bill.

Oh yeah, except for that.

It was a woman wearing a flowered dress, a bright pink cardigan, and a white sunhat. She smiled when Nat met her eyes.

"Hello."

"Hello," Nat replied, and resumed looking at her feet.

"Excuse me, miss?" the woman said.

Here it comes. Why are you wearing clothes that are ten sizes too big for you? How can you see with that hat over your eyes? Are you aware you look like the world's strangest farmer?

"Yeah?"

"Do you know what floor the cafeteria is on?"

"Third," Nat said, not knowing if it was true, and not caring. The doors opened on the parkade level, and she sauntered off into the gloom, pretending to search for her car until she was satisfied no one was watching.

Freedom. She was free.

The cab driver had grumbled about driving her out of town, and grumbled still louder when Nat explained her wallet had been stolen and she'd need to get money from whomever was at the house to pay him.

It had required taking off the oversized hat so he could see the bandages, her black eye and swollen cheeks in order to convince him.

"Geez. What happened to you?"

"Bar fight. You think this is bad, you should see the other guy."

The cabbie shook his head, probably imagining what he would tell his friends about the crazy woman he'd picked up two blocks from the hospital, but he unlocked the door. That was what mattered.

The thirty-minute drive over increasingly bumpy country roads that made the driver swear, quietly at first and then not so quietly, gave her time to consider her options. If the Tanners weren't there, and she suspected they weren't, she'd have to find a way into the house and pay them back for the damages later. They'd understand, and if they didn't, she'd almost died defending them. How angry at her could they rightfully be?

She was surprised to see a bunch of men she didn't recognize clustered on the front porch, kneeling in front of a steel door that looked better suited to a bank. *Wow, Riley is taking this home security thing seriously.* But why the door? The house was wall-to-wall windows. What was she going to do about those, brick the family inside?

"Are you sure this is the place?" the driver asked, eying the men, who were staring at them with expressions of obvious curiosity.

"Yep. Give me a minute. My purse is inside," she said, praying that it was, that the Tanners hadn't brought her things to the hospital. In that respect, hopefully her lack of clothes had been a good sign.

Nat pushed the hat's brim further up on her forehead as she approached the men, hoping they'd notice her injuries—how could they not?—and take pity on her. "Hello."

They nodded at her, looking suspicious.

"I need to get in there so I can pay this guy," she said, striving again for casual. She was thrilled to see the door they - had installed was open. "My purse is inside the house."

"Do you have any ID?" a man with white hair asked.

"I do, but it's in my purse. Which is in there." She pointed. "I'm a houseguest of the Tanners. I'm staying with Riley and Jason. And Brooke."

An intruder wouldn't know the family's names, right? *Right?*

The men exchanged a look. "Let me call Rod Silver," White Hair said. "If he says it's okay, then it's okay with me."

"But I don't know who that is. I'm staying with the Tanners."

"Rod is the real estate agent. He's the one who hired us. He will be able to get a hold of the family."

"Great, but can I pay him first?" She gestured at the cab driver, who was looking more irritated by the second. "One of you can come with me, make sure I don't take anything that isn't mine."

White Hair raised an eyebrow. "How will we know what's yours?"

"If my wallet is in my purse, and my purse is where I left it, I'll be able to show you my ID."

The man appeared to consider this while she squirmed. Then again, there was no hurry. If the cab driver got too impatient, he could take it up with this guy. *He* was the hold up, not her. "What do you think?" White Hair asked his buddies.

"If you're with her, it should be okay. I don't see as you have anything to lose—she can't nab anything if you're there," another man said, and winked at her. *Ugh.*

"What if she's a master criminal? Those folks can swipe your wallet right from your own pocket."

One thing about White Hair—he was definitely the stubborn type.

"If I were a master criminal, I hardly think I'd take a cab up here and announce myself to you."

"I dunno…maybe that's what you *want* us to believe. Maybe that's part of your act," he said, but she caught the glint in his eye. For fuck's sake, this was *fun* for him.

Taking deep breaths from her nose to avoid launching herself at the man's jugular, Nat struggled to get her temper under control. "Can I please get my purse?"

"Sure, girlie. C'mon in," White Hair said, gesturing for her to follow him into the house as if there'd never been a problem. He waved at the cabbie.

Girlie?

Never mind. She was in, and that's what mattered.

All the lights were off, and in the eastern side of the house, it was already too dark for her to see well. She didn't like being in the closed, dim-lit space with a strange man, but she didn't have a lot of choice. While he'd led the way initially, he now hung back, watching her.

He wants to see if I know where I'm going. Fine.

Pressing her hand against the wall, she managed to get to her room without walking into a table. The room looked exactly like she'd left it, thankfully. Riley hadn't had the time to bring her any belongings. Her purse was near the bed on the floor.

Nat grabbed it, groping for her wallet as White Hair stared at her. Her driver's license photo was enough to make her wince. It was of a pre-Dyatlov Nat, when her face had still had a childish roundness that she'd hated. She knew better now. This Nat was much more appealing than today's gaunt, sunken-eyed version. Although she hadn't been allowed to smile in the picture, she looked happy. Her eyes gleamed in a way they hadn't since Andrew died. Would White Hair even recognize her?

She thrust the identification at him, silently daring him to give her a tough time.

"This don' look much like you."

"That was a long time ago. But it's me. You have to see that."

He winked again. "Jus' having a bit of fun with you, girlie. Let's get that driver paid before he starts hollering up a storm. It's not good to leave people waiting."

Justifiable homicide. She was sure it would apply in this case.

After the driver had been paid and peeled out in the most dramatic fashion, Nat thanked the men for their lack of help and slipped back into the house before they could argue. Seeking the solace of her room, she closed the door and locked it before retreating to the bed to wait for the workmen to leave.

Home.

Or, as close as it got these days.

Lying on her back, she folded her hands across her stomach and stared up at the ceiling. *Okay, smart ass, what now?* Her head throbbed, and she worried about the damage she might have caused by leaving the hospital too early.

Steven was silent when it counted, as usual. *Figures.*

She closed her eyes.

Thump, thump, thump.

Nat bolted upright and then fell back against the pillows as a wave of dizziness hit her. She was surrounded by darkness, and it took her a moment to remember where she was.

Thump, thump, thump.

As the probable source of the sound occurred to her, her pulse quickened. Why would they have come back? The Tanners weren't here. It should look like *no one* was here. The chilling thought that the creatures must have been watching the house when she arrived was hard to bear.

Or maybe they could smell her.

That was worse.

Crouching, she tiptoed through the darkened house to the kitchen. Moonlight poured in through the repaired window, and she sucked in her breath.

A silhouette was cast on the opposite wall—a silhouette with an impossibly large, round head and curved shoulders, as if she'd given a child black paper and some scissors and asked for a cutout of a person.

But this was no person.

No one, aside from the tallest players in the NBA, could reach the top of that window frame without a ladder, and Nat doubted there were any basketball players skulking around this house in Oregon.

Thump, thump, thump.

She flinched, and then, angered at her reaction, steadied herself. She was not going to be intimidated by these creeps. That's exactly what they wanted. Though they didn't know it yet, *she* had the upper hand.

What they want is to kill you. Payback time for their Russian relatives.

She rejected the thought. As much as it pained her to admit, if they'd wanted to kill her, they could have. Her skull was fractured. A little more pressure, a little more force, and boom—no more Nat. There had been a time not so long ago when she would have welcomed that idea. But not anymore.

Not like this.

Could they honestly know what she'd done in Dyatlov? But how? Monstrous or not, they were animals. Animals didn't read the paper or watch the news. Had their instincts become so honed that they'd recognized her as a special threat? Or was it simply that she'd frightened or irritated them when she'd run outside with the shotgun?

But if that was the case, why hadn't they hurt Riley when she did the same thing?

Sitting on the floor where the creature…or *creatures*…couldn't see her, Nat rested her back and throbbing head against the wall and considered what she knew. Sasquatch, or Bigfoot, were generally thought to be gentle animals. The terror from seeing one resulted from their massive size, fierce appearance, and the body's natural adrenalin-surge reaction from experiencing something outside the realm of "normal" experience. In all the shows she'd conducted about Sasquatch sightings, there hadn't been a single report of anyone being harmed by one of the creatures. The scariest thing the animals had done was follow the witnesses, but more often than not, they took off as soon as they spotted people. More spooked rabbit than monster.

However, what she'd encountered in Dyatlov had been the furthest thing from gentle. They'd stalked the group, all right, but they'd done a hell of a lot more than stalk. There had been sophisticated sabotage, or at least it had appeared that way to Nat at the time, but now, with some space between her and the tragedy, she wondered. Other animals—monkeys, crows, jays—also "stole" objects from humans. These creatures were bigger, so it stood to reason that the objects they took would be bigger as well.

Had the intelligence she'd given them credit for been nothing more than instinct? All predatory animals could hunt and stalk their prey. There was no reason to believe these ones were superior to everything else they shared a forest with.

One thing she knew for certain: these creatures were *not* the same as the ones she'd encountered in Dyatlov. Yes, there were some similarities, but one difference overruled them all.

If they were the same, she'd be in much worse shape than she was.

She'd be dead.

CHAPTER FIFTEEN

"What about poison?"

"What *about* poison?" her mother asked, sounding annoyed.

"I get that you folks didn't like my idea of burning down the forest, and I guess I can understand that. Other creatures would be harmed, not just the ones causing you problems."

"Harmed? They'd be destroyed."

She felt like cheering for her mother. She'd hated that idea too. Even though the forest was sort of scary now, it was her favorite part of living in that house.

"Yes, yes," the old man said. She had found him frightening at first, with his gruff voice and his scowl, but she was glad her mom could stand up to him. "I get that. But poison could be more targeted, and that way, you wouldn't have to risk hurting other animals."

"What would we poison, exactly?" her dad asked. "We don't have a clue what they eat."

"You've seen their teeth. They're carnivores, right? Got to be, with teeth like that. Poison a few nice, juicy steaks, and boom!" Brooke jumped as the man clapped his hands, startling her. "No more Bigfoot problem."

Her father wasn't so easily convinced. "But other animals could easily eat the steak too…bears, wolves, owls. We might end up trading one pest for another, or killing off innocent wildlife. Not to mention it would be an expensive experiment. *We* don't even eat steak."

"These aren't your average animals, either," her mother added. "First, we're shooting at them, and then we're leaving free meat lying around the yard? I don't think they'd fall for it."

"Okay, fine, right, okay. If you're so smart, what do *you* propose? Let's hear your ideas. You must have come up with something while you were ripping mine to shreds."

"Franklin…" Beth said. She always tried to stop her husband from getting too upset. Brooke wondered if it got tiring sometimes, like forever trying to cheer up a cranky baby.

"What? I'm just trying to help, but I'm about at my wit's end. I don't know what else to suggest. Remember, our solution was to move. We never thought about how we could *stay* on the property with those things."

"They seem to avoid you," Beth said, presumably speaking to her father. "Is there another man, a family member maybe, who could stay with Riley and Brooke when you're at work?"

"We have no family in Oregon, but I doubt Riley would want someone looking over her shoulder all the time anyway…would you?"

"No. It's not a bad idea, but for this to work, we have to be able to regain our independence. We can't keep asking other people for help, like we did with Nat."

"This Nat," the old man said in a dismissive way, and Brooke crinkled her nose. He better not say anything mean about her, or she'd make him sorry. She wasn't going to let anyone talk smack about her friend. "What was her plan, anyway?"

Silence fell over the room. No one said anything for a while, but it wasn't in a good way, like when her family hung out together on Sundays, doing their own thing in the same room. She could feel the difference.

Finally, her mom spoke. "I honestly can't say. I don't believe she got a chance to come up with one before she was hurt. It happened so quickly."

The man snorted. "Some great Sasquatch hunter. She should have had a plan before she got there."

Before Brooke could yell at him, her mother defended Nat. "That's not what she is. She never claimed to be a hunter, or an expert, or to have any answers for us. We were barely able to convince her to come—Brooke ended up being the one who talked her into it. She wanted to help us, but she never promised anything."

"But you're paying her, aren't you?"

"Of course we're paying her. We couldn't expect her to do this on her dime. Two weeks ago, she had no idea who we were. Why would she try to help us for free?"

"I don't understand. If she isn't a hunter or an expert, why did you call her? What could she possibly offer you?" The old man wouldn't give up, but that was okay. He didn't know Nat. If he'd met her, he'd get it right away.

"She has experience with these creatures—or, creatures like them, which is more than most people can say. It's not like you can look up Sasquatch hunters online." Her mom was getting fed up. Brooke could tell by the sound of her voice. Her mom didn't get mad often, but when she did, watch out.

The man harrumphed. "What you need is a SWAT team; that's what I think."

"I know you like Nat, honey, but Franklin may have a point. The first time she saw the creatures, she confronted them with a shotgun and nearly got herself killed. She might cause more harm than good, assuming she's ever strong enough to come back."

Oh, Dad. How could you?

"She was having a flashback, okay? It's easy for all of you to sit in judgment of her, but you have no idea what she's been through. She's faced creatures like this before, creatures who killed her colleagues and friends, and she was the only survivor. I trust her a lot more than I trust any one of you."

Go Mom! Nat hadn't been the only survivor, though. Brooke had learned that through her research.

"We weren't judging her at all. But if she's having flashbacks, our house is probably the worst place for her," her dad said, in that gentle, let's-all-calm-down tone he used to stop arguments. There were days, when she was really mad or frustrated, that she hated that tone. Her dad was always so calm, so reasonable. Sometimes she wished he'd get mad too.

"Why don't we let Nat make that decision for herself? She's a grown woman."

"A grown woman who almost died," said the old man.

"Argh," she said, and Brooke could picture her mom raising her hands in the air like she did whenever she lost a game of Scrabble. "I give up."

"Why don't we stop fighting with each other, and get back to thinking of ideas?" Beth asked. "Brooke thinks very highly of this Nat, and that's enough for me."

"Thank you." Her mom sounded relieved, and Brooke smiled. She liked Beth a lot. She was *so* much nicer than her husband.

"That SWAT team comment might have some potential," her dad said. "Well, not actually a SWAT team, but what if we got the police involved? They have the fire power we don't."

"The police department in Longview is strictly amateur hour. I don't think they'd help you much, and that's if they believed you. If the creature doesn't come around while you're home, they'd probably hide from the police too. And if it did show up, the cops might end up no better than your friend."

"You have a point, Frank. Or do you prefer Franklin?" her dad asked.

"Either is fine. Would you like another beer?"

"I'd better quit when I'm ahead, but thanks."

"Suit yourself. Riley?"

"Sure, I'll have another. Why not? All this arguing has made me thirsty."

She chose that moment to make her entrance, rubbing her eyes as if she'd awoken from a sound sleep. She wasn't sure how the grown-ups would feel if they found out she'd been listening to their conversation. "Mom?"

"Brooke, what are you doing up?" Her mom's face was flushed a bright pink, but whether that was from the fighting or the beer, she wasn't sure. "You should have been in bed a long time ago."

"I was, but I couldn't sleep."

"Oh dear…is there something wrong with the bed? Is it not comfortable?" Beth asked, a dismayed expression on her face, and Brooke felt bad. She should have said something else, something closer to the truth—that sleeping was scary.

"I'm sure it's fine. Brooke's been having a lot of nightmares lately." Her mom put an arm around her shoulders. "Is that what it was, another nightmare?"

Seeing an out, she nodded. "I think so."

As Franklin put another beer in front of her mother—she didn't miss the nasty look Beth gave him (was there something wrong with beer?)—she decided it was time to speak up, which was why she'd announced her presence in the first place. "I heard what you guys were talking about."

"Did you? Oh, honey, we were being silly."

"No, you weren't. He wants to kill them." She pointed at the old man, though she'd been taught that pointing was rude. He ignored her, and that was rude too.

"I don't think anyone wants to kill anyone. But we don't have the money to move right now, so we have to figure out something."

"But—why do they have to die? Why do we have to kill them?"

"There's a saying in this world, girl—*kill or be killed.* Sometimes you have to fight back," the old man said. "I'm beginning to wish we had, but we honestly didn't have it in us."

"But they haven't done anything wrong." She bit her lip to stop it from trembling, feeling dangerously on the verge of tears but unsure why.

"They hurt Nat," her dad said, but his eyes were kind. She didn't think he wanted to kill them, either. Not so long ago, he hadn't even believed in them.

"I know, but they were scared. She went out there with a gun. They were protecting themselves."

The old man made a huffing noise, but her mom glared at him. "Actually, what she's saying is true. For the most part, they've only gotten aggressive when they've been confronted—or seen my shotgun. The rest of their behavior *could* be explained away as curiosity."

"What about the door? They ripped the door off its hinges." Her dad frowned, but Brooke understood he was worried for them, about leaving them alone when he left for work. She was worried too.

"Maybe they were upset about what Nat did," she said. She turned to her mother. "Remember when the bear almost got me and Nat? You didn't shoot the bear."

"What?" Her dad's mouth gaped, his eyes widening, and she saw he hadn't known.

"I would have, honey, but I couldn't shoot it without hurting you or Nat." Her mother held her close for a moment. "I'll tell you later," she said to her dad. "There's been so much going on, I honestly forgot."

"But you're not talking about how to kill the bear," Brooke said. Why were adults so hard to talk to? She'd thought her point was fairly obvious. "The bear could have hurt us, but you're not worried about it."

"I *am* worried about it. It wasn't acting right. With replacing the door and coming here, I'd forgotten. But we're probably going to need to do something about that too," her mom said. "We don't want it to be unsafe for you to go outside."

Her dad sighed, covering his eyes with a hand. "Great. Anything else I should know about?"

"I think I understand what Brooke is trying to say," Beth said, smiling at her. "The incident with the bear was scary, but we're not talking about killing it because bears are wild animals, and we accept that wild animals are sometimes aggressive. But these creatures are wild animals too, and the only time they've been aggressive has been when they've felt threatened. Do I have that about right, dear?"

Brooke nodded, relieved. Thankfully one adult understood her. "Why do they have to die? Why can't we share the woods with them?"

She couldn't say it to the adults, because they'd think she was weird, but sometimes she hated being human. Humans destroyed everything. They didn't seem able to live with any other wild creature without attempting to control it. Her teacher often talked about all the ways people were wrecking the world, and it made her cry. She felt so helpless a lot of the time—she was just a kid, what could she do? But with her parents, maybe she *could* do something. Maybe they would listen to her before they set fire to the woods, or threw a bunch of poisoned meat all over the place.

"That's a great idea, honey," her dad said. "But we have to consider the fact that they may not want to share them with us."

* * *

She had to use her brain. That is, whatever was left of it.

Once the pounding on the window ceased, Nat had found an ice pack in the Tanners' freezer, and held it to her head. It didn't make the throbbing go away, but it eased the intensity.

She kept the lights off. The creatures remained near the house, circling. Every now and then, she heard an unnatural rustling, or a scraping against the windows. It made her flinch each time, but there was no attempt to break in, no cracking of the glass or growling and snarling. If they knew she was there, they obviously weren't *that* motivated to kill her. It would have been simple enough for them to break the front window and finish what they'd started.

Think, Nat, think.

In Dyatlov, she'd gone on the offensive. She'd used everything she had to fight back, including her strength. But that wasn't an option, not anymore. Her head injury made her extremely fragile. She was going to have to use her wits.

She could imagine what Steven would say about that, what obvious jib he would make about her being half-witted. But he continued his silence, and she questioned whether he had ever been there at all. Had it truly been Steven convincing her to leave, or a part of her injured brain understanding she needed something outside herself to guide her?

The Riordans had left the house like thieves fleeing in the night, selling the place for an unbelievable price. So, the Tanners weren't the first family to experience something threatening or frightening here. Whatever the creatures' intentions, they avoided the house when Jason was home, but why? From what Nat had experienced, there was no reason for the beasts to be scared of or intimidated by the man of the house. They could throw him around as easily as they had her.

They'd had many opportunities to kill a member of the family. When Riley charged outside with her gun, and Brooke had called for her, screaming. After the attack on her, when Riley and Brooke had risked their lives to bring her inside. Once the creatures had ripped off the door, they could have hidden inside the house, waiting. The very thought made her shudder. The point was, if their goal was to kill or otherwise hurt the family, there'd been no shortage of opportunities.

So, if they didn't want to kill the family, what *did* they want? Was it curiosity? Nat wasn't so sure about that, either. The Tanners were nice people, but she wouldn't call them endlessly fascinating. How exciting could looking in the same kitchen window, night after night, be? Even animals got used to changes in their environment and either accepted them or left after a while. Nat hadn't played their game, had stayed out of sight, and hadn't responded to the banging on the window, but they still knew she was there—or that someone was. They hadn't gone away. If they were nocturnal, which it appeared they were, they'd have a few hours left to hunt. Why were they wasting them watching the house? What were they after?

"It's something about the house," Nat whispered. "It's got to be."

Was it the house's existence? The Tanners' home truly was a "cabin in the woods." A large segment of forest would have been clear cut for its construction. Had the creatures' home been destroyed in the process? Were they unwilling to let humans live in peace because *their* peace had been ruined?

She felt she was getting somewhere closer to the truth. Animals tended to become a "problem" for humankind when humans encroached upon their territory, not the other way around. The bears who wandered into campsites, the wolves that killed pet dogs and chickens, the elephants that trampled gardens in Africa. In every case, people blamed the animals, but if they hadn't invaded the animals' territory, those clashes would happen rarely, or not at all.

We're a virus, she thought, and not for the first time.

It was painful to contemplate, but had it been the same with Dyatlov? Had they invaded the creatures' territory, threatening them? Had they reacted on instinct, determined to rid their world of these smelly, messy people before more arrived and set up camp?

It had *felt* like more. It had felt personal, malicious. But then again, humans tended to take everything personally. That didn't mean they were right.

If it was the very existence of the house that was the problem, there wasn't much the Tanners could do. It was here, and they were stuck with it—Jason had made that much pretty clear. Even if the family moved, that wouldn't resolve the situation for the next people, and damned if she ever wanted to come back here to help another family. Once was enough.

Her thought that the animals adapted to changes in their environment seemed too simple of an explanation. Something about the house kept drawing them back, no matter who lived here. But *what*?

One thing's for certain: she wasn't going to find out by hiding in the dark, holding an icepack to her forehead.

Staggering to her feet, Nat crept out of the room, determined to do some digging.

CHAPTER SIXTEEN

Where do you begin a search when you have no idea what you're looking for?

Nat decided to take her cue from the creatures themselves. For some reason, they appeared to be drawn repeatedly to the kitchen. Although the living area had the largest windows, and they could have settled themselves at a discreet distance and watched the Tanners as if the family was their own private entertainment, it was the kitchen's windows they pounded on.

Why?

Nothing about the kitchen was unusual or striking. Its walls were the same golden logs as the rest of the house. Whoever had designed it had understood a thing or two about cooking—every convenience that made life easier for a cook was in evidence: the undercabinet lighting, the movable island with storage drawers, the magnetic knife rack.

And yet, the Sasquatch kept pounding on this window as if they were trying to lead Riley and Brooke here. *Why?* What was it about this room?

The obvious answer was food. Were the creatures starving? Could they smell the contents of the fridge?

Feeling silly, she opened the refrigerator door, hoping the light didn't unleash another flurry of pounding.

Wow.

The state of the family's fridge was worse than hers.

Either the Tanners had taken most of the food with them on the road, Riley hadn't gone shopping for a while, or they were dead broke.

Nat recognized the signs. A few cans of beer, a loaf of white bread, some apples they'd picked from their own trees, and half a package of bologna. Instead of a family of three, this was the fridge of a college dude living off a loan. Yikes.

That settled it. Whatever had attracted the Sasquatch, it was definitely not in the fridge. Nat was starving, and nothing in there tempted her—except perhaps the beer. This time, though, her mouth hadn't watered. Progress.

She sniffed the air. Curious—there was a smell in here she hadn't noticed before. For a moment, she thought it was something in the fridge that had gone off, but this was a musty smell—earthy, like you'd sometimes get in a basement.

The basement had been the one part of the house Brooke hadn't shown her during the grand tour. "I don't like going down there," the girl had said, wrinkling her nose. "It smells funny and it's dark."

She hadn't thought anything of it, because what kid likes basements? She'd hated the one in her childhood home, always felt like something chased her when she ran back up the stairs. But now it had potential. Maybe the "funny smell" was attractive to Sasquatch, who knows?

It smells funny and it's dark....

Retrieving her cell from where she'd left it on the floor, Nat engaged the flashlight app and made her way to the basement door. So far, so good. The Sasquatch either hadn't noticed the meagre sources of light she'd been using, or they had decided to give her a break.

She was betting on the former.

The door to the basement was closed, as always. Opening it, she prepared to be hit with a wave of unpleasant smells—the reek of stagnant water or mold-encrusted walls, but there was nothing.

Shining the light from her phone to see as much as she could, she immediately understood why Brooke didn't care for it. The lovely golden logs from upstairs were gone; here, the walls were comprised of some kind of stone block with either mud or a concrete mixture holding them together. The overall effect was drab and gloomy, as if the basement sucked in every speck of light and spit out darkness in return.

A massive spiderweb blocked the entrance, complete with several trapped bugs in various stages of death and decay. When was the last time anyone had been down here? It wasn't picturesque, but the laundry room had to be here, right? Ducking under the web, Nat crouched to get down the stairs, but was hit with a rush of dizziness and nearly lost her balance. Heart pounding, she clutched the railing until she caught her breath.

She had to be more careful. Never mind being mauled by Sasquatch. If she lost her balance and tumbled down the stairs, hitting her head, that would be the end of her.

During her almost-fall, she'd squeezed her phone and the flashlight had gone off, leaving her in darkness. Nat felt the same pressure she'd experienced in the basement of her childhood home—that creepy-crawly sensation that something was down there, watching her.

What if one of the creatures *had* remained in the home? What if it was down here, hiding?

Don't be ridiculous. You'd hear it breathe.

Yet, there was something wrong with this place. She didn't think it was her imagination.

"Turn on my flashlight."

"It's on," her version of the phone's intelligent assistant said, his voice startling in the empty (hopefully empty) basement.

Holding onto the railing, she carefully made her way down the remainder of the steps to the concrete floor. The musty smell was stronger here, but not too bad. Despite her near-death experience on the stairs, this was an ordinary basement. The realization gave her a sinking feeling of disappointment. It wasn't like she'd *wanted* to find anything spooky down there, but if she didn't find any answers as to why the creatures were so fixated on this house, she wouldn't be able to help the Tanners. She was surprised to find she wanted to help them, especially Brooke. It had been a long time since she'd mustered up the energy to care about anyone.

Dusty shelves lined the walls to her right, containing some old sporting equipment and what looked to be a Christmas tree in a storage bag. On her left were three rooms, their closed doors daring her.

"All right, let's see what's behind door number one," she said, almost wishing Steven would answer her. She might be tempted to listen to him this time.

Behind door number one was a bathroom with a shower. It was clean and bright, with white fixtures. Obviously a new addition, but hopefully not intended as a guest bath. Who would want to stay down here?

Behind door number two was the expected laundry room. Cramped and grimy, but someone had made an attempt to clean it up. *Riley?* An overflowing clothes basket waited on top of the dryer.

Nothing to see here.

As she opened door number three, the stench struck her with such an intensity that she took several steps back. Holding her arm across her face, as if that could possibly protect her nose, she peered inside.

"What the hell is *that?*"

The odor had an echo of the mustiness she'd detected upstairs, but it was much, much worse. Something had rotted or died in this room, maybe several somethings, from the smell of it. Not wanting to know, but accepting she had no choice, Nat held her breath and shone the light into the room.

To her relief, no corpse—animal or otherwise—awaited her. It was just another small, nondescript room with a concrete floor. She couldn't tell what its purpose had been, as the room was empty. Noticing her light didn't reach the back wall of the room, she stepped inside, breathing through her mouth. The fetor increased to the point where it was overwhelming. For a moment, Nat worried she would throw up.

She soon saw where the stink was emanating from: at the back of the room was a crawl space with water pipes running along its top. It had to be located below the kitchen sink. Had the sink flooded, or leaked, and stale water was causing this smell? Nat knew that could get fairly rank, but not *this* rank. No, that wouldn't be the cause of this. There had to be something else. Had an old garbage disposal malfunctioned and strewn food waste down here?

Her chest tightened so much she could barely take a breath, which—considering the atmosphere—might have been a blessing.

"The things I get myself into," she muttered, wishing she'd never had this bright idea in the first place.

The crawl space had a dirt floor, which explained the earthy mustiness, but it wasn't empty. It appeared to be crammed full of rocks and other debris. And…something else?

Nat stuck her hand in the space and shone the light around, hoping to get a better look. What was that stuff?

Though most of it was coated with dirt, every now and then, a bit of white shone through. Stiffening, she finally recognized what she was staring at.

Oh, shit.

* * *

The chatter of cheerful voices, a most unfamiliar sound, awakened him. Franklin groaned, and groped for his alarm clock. Nine a.m. Hardly an indecent hour, but he'd definitely overslept.

His head ached something awful. Never a morning person at the best of times, it took a few minutes for the fog to clear so he could figure out what was wrong. Ah, yes—the beer. Too. Much. Beer. Beth wasn't going to be happy with him today. Oh well. Some sacrifices were worth the suffering. How long had it been since he'd had someone to drink with? He'd enjoyed sparring with Riley. She had a lot of spirit. Her husband seemed like a nice enough guy too, though he could stand to relax a little.

The phone rang, its shrill yelp aggravating his headache. One thing he and Beth *had* agreed on—no cell phones. They hated the damn contraptions, just another way for the government to spy on you. Who needed it? In his day, people could be unavailable now and then, and everyone accepted it. Why did anyone need to have a damn phone attached to their hip night and day? Unless you were a doctor or a cop, there was no excuse.

Still, cell phones had an advantage that landlines didn't— their ring didn't make an already miserable headache worse.

"Franklin?"

Beth's features blurred as he struggled to bring them into focus. "Yeah?" His voice was raspy, and sounded harsher than he'd intended. But if he'd offended her, she didn't show it.

"There's a call I think you should take."

He groaned again, rubbing his pounding forehead. "I'm not feeling so great."

"I'm not surprised. I keep telling you this is what happens, but you never listen to me."

"Yeah, yeah. Please save the lecture for when my head isn't falling apart."

"You need to take this call."

The last thing he wanted at that moment was a person speaking directly into his ear. His stomach churned, and he burped, tasting old beer and bile. Nasty. "Can't you handle it?"

"They want to talk to you, and I think that would be best."

Putting a hand on the night table, he pushed himself into a sitting position. This didn't do his head any favors. "I think I'm going to be sick."

"*Please*, Frank. It's important."

He raised his watery eyes to hers, accepting defeat. "Well, at least tell me who this oh-so-important caller is."

"It's the police from Longview. Hurry. They're going to think I hung up on them."

Maybe that wouldn't be such a bad idea. Would give him some time to think. His mind was racing. What would Longview Police want with them? Had Riley and Jason decided to sue them after all? But that would be ludicrous. They hadn't done anything illegal. They were on murky *moral* ground, perhaps, but no one in this country passed out prison sentences for that. "What do they want?"

"They want to talk to you about the house."

"The house? Because of this Bigfoot business?" It didn't make any sense. The whole confounded town knew about it, and had known about it for some time—why would they be making a fuss about it now?

She hesitated, holding onto the door frame. "No, I don't think so. I don't think this has anything to do with that."

"Then *what*?" Was she deliberately trying to drive him crazy, or did she do it naturally?

"They found something at the house, Frank." To his horror, he saw her eyes were full of tears. "Something bad. Something *really* bad."

CHAPTER SEVENTEEN

The lights swirled over the ground, painting the grass sickly colors. Nat sat on the porch in a daze, watching as the cops hurried in and out of the house, rarely sparing her a glance—which was fine with her.

"Ma'am?"

The officer hovering above her looked friendly enough. Her ponytail reminded Nat briefly of Brooke. Ugh, the Tanners. She owed them a big apology: for snooping around and inadvertently turning their home into a crime scene, and for not letting them know she'd left the hospital. Staff at Longview General had alerted Riley that morning, and she had called Nat, absolutely frantic. The list of things Nat had to atone for was getting longer.

"Call me Nat, please." She couldn't stand being addressed as ma'am. It never failed to make her feel old.

"Nat it is. Are you all right? You look like you've been on the wrong end of a beating. Would you like me to take you to the hospital?"

After I did all that hard work to escape? "Thanks, but no thanks. I'll be okay."

She nodded, in that crisp way cops have, jotting down a note. *Crazy woman refuses hospital treatment, even though it looks like she's been mauled by a bear*, most likely. "Would you like to press charges against whoever did this to you?"

Nat nearly laughed at the thought. "I don't think you'd have much luck with that. All of this…" she gestured to her face and the bandages covering her head, "…is the result of a run-in with the local wildlife."

"The local wildlife?" The cop raised an eyebrow.

"Yes, the local *wildlife*." Nat waited for a reaction, for any hint of recognition on the officer's face. But either there was none, or the woman was a fabulous actress.

"Whatever it was, it must have had a hell of a punch."

"It did. Cracked my skull open."

The cop glanced up from her notepad, looking so startled it was comical. "Are you sure you shouldn't be in the hospital?"

"I probably should be, but I'll heal faster on the outside. As long as I don't have to go back in there." She hooked her thumb at the house, hoping the woman would understand she meant the basement.

"No, you won't have to go back in there. No one but us is going to be allowed to go back in there for a while."

Great. The Tanners would be thrilled to hear that. This house may have not turned out the way they'd hoped, but at least it had been a place to lay their heads at night. "Were you able to get a hold of them?"

Another nod. "They're on their way. You were house sitting for them while they were in Arizona?"

Close enough. "Yes."

"There was some confusion when we reached them. I believe they said something about you being in the hospital."

"I *was* in the hospital, but I left. I hadn't had a chance to let them know yet."

"How well do you know the Tanners, ma—Nat?"

"Not that well. I met them a couple of weeks ago." She looked up sharply at the cop as she grasped the probable reason for the question. "If you're asking if the Tanners did...*that*, not a chance."

"How are you so sure, if you don't know them that well?"

"I just am. You get a feeling about people, especially in my line of work, and that family is good people."

"Your line of work? What is it that you do?"

"I host a podcast."

"Oh? Which one? I love podcasts," the cop said, appearing to be genuinely interested.

"*Nat's Mysterious World.*" Nat hoped the woman had never heard of it, but saw immediately that this was not a day when any of her wishes would be granted.

"I've heard that one a few times. It's a good show." A light went on behind the woman's eyes. "Now I understand why you're here."

Uh oh. "You do?"

"Sure, you're the one that investigates UFOs and sea monsters, right?"

She wasn't sure *investigates* was the right word, but whatever. "I used to."

"You must be here for Bigfoot. Sure you are. It makes sense. Longview holds the record for Sasquatch sightings, and you're staying at the Monster House." Catching herself, the woman looked over her shoulder as if afraid someone else had overheard. "Guess it really is the Monster House now."

Nat smiled, though it felt like the most unnatural expression in the world, given the circumstances. "Are they real?"

She knew the answer, though. Of course she did. There could be no other explanation for that gruesome smell.

The cop's jaw tightened. "They're real, yes. Unfortunately."

"Are they...human?"

"I'm sorry, but I'm not at liberty to reveal that information at this time." There'd been a flicker, though. Something in the eyes. Enough to give Nat her answer.

"Can you tell me again how you found them?"

"I smelled something awful coming from the basement, and decided to see what it was."

One of the many, many times she wished she'd minded her own damn business.

"Had you been down there before?"

"No. I haven't been staying here that long, and then I got hurt." She gestured at her head. "I don't know if the Tanners have been down there much. They bought the house not that long ago."

"They sounded pretty shocked when we called them," the cop admitted. "Mrs. Tanner didn't seem to be aware of which room we were referring to."

"I'm not surprised. They've had a lot of other things to deal with." *Shut up, Nat—unless you want to impress the officer with your firsthand knowledge of the local wildlife.* "Moving in, finding a job, and stuff like that. And Jason—her husband—is usually on the road."

The cop covered her mouth with a fist and coughed. "Maybe it's because I'm in law enforcement, but I can't imagine not noticing a smell like that. I would have ripped that place apart trying to find the cause."

"Honestly, yesterday is the first time I noticed it, and only after a while, and only when standing near the kitchen sink. Otherwise, I didn't smell anything out of the ordinary. Even last night, it just smelled musty."

Until she'd gotten close enough, and then...

It was better not to think about that. She didn't want to get sick again.

"Looks to me like the whole thing used to be covered up, but some of the dirt shifted over time. Maybe that's why no one found it until now. The former owners, the—" she checked her notes, "—Riordans, they claim they never noticed anything either."

"I believe it. I get that it must sound impossible, given the way it is now, but I swear it wasn't that bad even yesterday."

She nodded again, but whether she actually believed Nat was anyone's guess. "Do you have any idea where you'll be staying? We're going to need to contact you for an official statement."

Where she'd be staying...yikes. That was the other big question of the day. Should she go home? That is, if that was an option now? She'd been counting on the Tanners to pay for her return flight, but she couldn't hold them to that, not after this new development. No one would. For the time being, the creatures would be the least of their worries.

Her panic must have shown, because the cop said, "We have an account at the Longview Inn. We could put you up there for the night, until the Tanners get back and you're able to figure something else out."

Relief washed over her, along with gratitude for the officer's kindness. "That would be great, thanks."

"Just give us your word you won't leave town until we get your statement."

So much for going home. "Sure, I promise. Do you know when that will be?"

"I imagine tomorrow." The cop checked her cell. "I need to finish up a few things here, but if you don't mind waiting, I can give you a ride to the inn. Or, I could call you a cab. Whichever you prefer."

"I don't mind waiting. Thanks, officer." Maybe, if the officer got to trust her, she'd reveal more about what Nat had found in the basement.

"Not a problem. Can I get you anything?"

She lifted the bottle of water another cop had given her. "I'm good for now."

"Okay. Hang tight and I'll be back in a few. Oh, and Nat?"

"Yes."

"Please keep this to yourself for now. I don't mind you talking to the Tanners, but that's it. No media, no friends and family. Not until we give you the all-clear. Okay?"

That one was easy. She didn't have much in the way of friends or family these days. And media? She'd rather face a firing squad.

Besides, how could she tell anyone what she'd found when she wasn't sure what it was?

* * *

That night, she returned to the basement.

The stench was worse. It permeated everything, making it difficult to breathe.

Crime scene tape fell to the ground at her approach, whispering against the concrete.

Against the rank dirt of the crawl space gleamed something white. Nat cringed, and tried to pull away, tried to keep from reliving the nightmare of her gruesome find.

But this time she saw what she'd missed.

A skull, small enough to balance on her palm.

The skull of a child.

Loud pounding startled her out of a fitful sleep. *What the—?* She was positive she'd put out the *Do Not Disturb* sign. Through bleary eyes, she checked her cell for the time. 10:00 a.m. She'd actually slept through the night. Over ten hours.

She was a terrible person. Who could sleep after what she'd found?

The overzealous housekeeping staff pounded on the door again.

"Go away; I don't want any," she yelled, burying her throbbing head in a pillow.

"Nat?"

The familiar voice was the last thing she'd expected. Grateful that she'd fallen asleep in her clothes—again—she hurried to the door as fast as her condition would allow.

Her visitors looked worse than she felt, if that were possible, but to Nat, they were the proverbial sight for sore eyes. Inexplicably, she felt like weeping as Brooke enveloped her in a ferocious hug.

"Careful, honey," Riley cautioned. "She's still hurt."

"It's fine," Nat said, and it was. She stroked the girl's hair, relieved that Brooke was there, and okay. But why wouldn't she be? Some residual bad energy from her nightmare had caused her to fear for the girl's safety.

"Sorry to barge in on you like this," Jason said. "But when we found out you weren't at the hospital anymore, we freaked."

She winced. *Shit.* She should have told them. She'd *meant* to tell them. But in all the confusion, it had completely slipped whatever was left of her mind.

"Come in." Letting go of Brooke to open the door wider, Nat kicked the tray holding the remnants of yesterday's lunch and dinner to the side. "Please."

Brooke clung to her, but her parents were more cautious, peering into the room as if they expected something to jump out and bite them.

"Are you sure? You look like you were sleeping. We tried calling first, but couldn't get an answer," Riley said.

"Of course I'm sure. Do you have any idea how good it is to see you guys?" The Tanners didn't know her, not really. They'd bonded through a traumatic experience, but the Tanners had no idea how long it had been since she'd been happy to see anyone.

Riley took her husband's hand. They lingered in the doorway, looking uncomfortable. *Why are they acting so weird? Is it because I was the one who found it?* She didn't believe for a second that the Tanners had anything to do with the bones in the basement, but it would be fantastic if they'd stop acting so goddamn guilty.

Nat waved them toward the unused bed. "Please, come in. Sit." Pulling the blanket over the place she'd been sleeping, she then sat on the bed across from them. Brooke immediately sat beside her. The child's presence made everything better.

Together, her parents perched on the edge of the other mattress, practically squirming.

"What's going on? You can't possibly believe I did it—there hasn't been enough time."

Riley smiled, but her lips quivered. "Of course we don't think you're responsible. But you're probably wondering about us."

Nat cast a meaningful look in Brooke's direction, but Jason was the one to answer. "She knows. Well, she knows as much as we do. Which admittedly isn't much. Hopefully the cops will start shedding some light on this soon."

"You can both relax," Nat said. "I don't think you had a thing to do with this. The thought didn't cross my mind for a second."

She used to think she was an excellent judge of character, but Dyatlov had proven her wrong, time and time again. Still, she was more likely to believe *she* was responsible for the bones than the Tanners. These were good people. That was one of the few things she was sure of.

At her words, Riley and Jason's shoulders sagged, as if between them they'd been supporting an impossible weight. "That's such a relief. We weren't sure you'd want to see us. We really wrestled with whether or not to come over here, especially when you weren't answering your phone," Riley said.

"I talked them into it," Brooke added.

"I'm glad you did. It's been pretty lonely around here." She put an arm around the kid and gave her a half-hug, ignoring the responding spike of pain in her head.

"Are you okay?" Riley asked. "Why did you leave the hospital?"

"That's a long story. I guess the simplest answer is that I felt I was running out of time. I needed to get back to the house and figure things out," she said. "The guys installing the new door let me in once I showed them my ID." It seemed like a lifetime ago.

"It looks like that bandage could stand to be changed." Riley frowned with concern. "I can do that for you."

"Thanks. I'm really sorry I didn't let you know. Everything happened pretty fast, and to be honest, I was afraid you'd have talked me out of it."

"Damn straight we would have talked you out of it. What's happening at the house isn't important. Not compared to this." Jason gestured at her head. "You should have stayed in the hospital."

Should I be honest? Nat wrestled with how much to tell them, but it was a short skirmish. She had a feeling the Tanners would understand. "To be honest, I couldn't afford to be in the hospital in the first place. My insurance isn't exactly in good standing."

She met Riley's eyes. "I know June told you some of what happened to me, or at least what she'd read in the media, because what I'd told you was the truth—I haven't spoken to her in years. But I was a real mess when you called. I've been a mess since that happened to me, since I've been back in the States. I'm afraid it might be a permanent condition."

Nat laughed, not surprised to hear how shaky and false it sounded. There was nothing funny about any of it, not really.

"What are you talking about? You're hardly a mess. You're the strongest person we've ever met, surviving something like that." Riley reached across the space between them to squeeze her hand. "Most of us wouldn't have made it this far."

"You're assuming I did. What if I told you it was a friend's ghost who talked me into leaving the hospital?" She braced herself for their reaction, but she'd decided there would be no more secrets. Secrets always did more harm than good.

Steven wasn't really a friend, but there wasn't enough time to explain their complicated relationship.

Rather than look at her like she'd gone mad, the Tanners didn't appear the least bit taken aback. "Nat, your skull has been fractured. I imagine anything you see or hear right now is completely normal, until you heal," Riley said.

"Or maybe it *was* a ghost," Brooke chimed in. "I believe in ghosts."

"I'm starting to," Nat said.

"As for the insurance, don't worry about that. We'll figure it out." Jason pushed his cap back and rubbed his forehead. "Seems like we're in the same boat where money's concerned. But insurance we have."

"Do you want to go back to the hospital?" Riley asked. "You probably should. A fractured skull is nothing to fool around with."

Wise words. Sage advice. Two things she'd never been any good at heeding. "Honestly, I think I'll be okay. It was a relief to get out of there. I'll just be as careful as I can."

Jason snorted. "And your idea of being careful was to go back to *our* house. Yeah, right."

Maybe they knew her better than she thought. "I guess no one is going back to your house for a while, huh?"

"Not for a few days at least. What *did* you find, Nat? The police have been incredibly evasive."

Looking over at Brooke again, Nat hesitated, but the girl encouraged her to go on. "It's okay," she said. "I can take it. Not knowing is the worst."

Got that right. Seeing her parents weren't objecting, Nat took a deep breath and forced herself to return to the basement, if only in her mind. "Bones. I found bones. In the crawl space under the kitchen sink. I was standing in the kitchen, after the...after the creatures had left, and I smelled something bad...something rotting. I decided to see if I could find out what it was. God knows what I was thinking, but my curiosity has always been a curse." She studied Riley and Jason's faces, suddenly realizing what she sounded like. "I wasn't snooping, I swear. I poked around in the basement, nowhere else."

"Hey, that's okay. We trust you," Riley said. She leaned her head on her husband's shoulder. "It's so hard to believe this is happening, on top of everything else. How didn't we see this? Why didn't we notice anything?"

"Neither of us have spent a hell of a lot of time in the basement. I know the room you're talking about, and I didn't store anything in there. I never liked the way it smelled." This time he removed his cap to run his hand through his hair. "Though I never imagined it was caused by anything like *that*. The thought gives me the creeps—to think that we were living above something like that, and had no clue."

"It was easy to miss. They were pretty well hidden," Nat said. "At first, all I saw was something white, but once I started brushing the dirt away—well, I thought it best to get the hell out of there and call the police."

"Were you scared?" Brooke asked. "I would have been so scared."

She thought for a moment. There had been a time when she would have sworn nothing could scare her again. But life had a way of throwing her nasty surprises. She remembered how it had felt, finding the bones in that dark basement and feeling the pressure, as if the entire house was watching her, waiting to see what she would do. "Yes, I was. Terrified. But we don't know what the bones *are*. They could have come from an animal."

"That's what we're hoping," Jason said. "For obvious reasons, but also so we can get back into the house. Not that we *want* to, but our options are a bit limited right now."

Nat saw the fear on his face and rushed to reassure him. "Don't worry about the money. I have a few credit cards with some room on them. We'll take advantage of Longview's hospitality for as long as they're willing to give it, and then I'll cover the cost."

"We can't let you do that," Riley said. "We're supposed to be paying *you*."

"We'll figure it out," Nat echoed Jason. "Remember, we're in the same boat."

It was bizarre to feel optimistic, considering the situation. Aggressive Sasquatches outside, unidentified bones inside. But she *did* feel optimistic, and it felt good. It had been a long time since she'd faced a day feeling anything other than dread.

"We'll pay you back, however long it takes. I'll be taking on more trips as soon as I know it's safe. I'll pile on the overtime," Jason said, and she was sorry for him. She could barely keep her own life in order, and the poor guy was responsible for three. It was obvious how much it weighed on him. He'd aged overnight.

"Honestly, don't worry about it. It will work out. How was Arizona? Did you find out anything? How were the Riordans?"

"They were nice people. Couldn't tell us much though." Jason sighed.

"Except for the old man." Brooke wrinkled her nose. "I didn't like him. He was mean. He wanted us to set fire to the forest and kill all the animals."

Nat made a face. "Lovely. Somehow, I don't think that's the answer."

"He was a little gruff, but I got the feeling he was worried about his wife, and how she would handle us showing up on her doorstep," Riley said. "They were both concerned when they saw Brooke with us, said they'd made Rod Silver promise not to sell the house to anyone with children."

"They treated us well," Jason added. "Can't complain. I can't say how I would have acted in their position. They thought they were free of this damn mess. And now this newest development has them reeling."

"They didn't know about the bones?" Nat asked.

He shook his head. "Not a thing. They're as much in the dark as we are."

"That girl in the library had it right," Riley said. "It *is* the Monster House."

Despair nibbled at the edges of her optimism. Though she'd known it was unlikely the Riordans would have been able to tell them anything useful—if they'd had the answers, they probably wouldn't have fled town—she'd hoped for better than this. "They didn't give you anything?"

"They did tell us the creatures weren't aggressive when they were living in the house. They were frightening, but it seemed like they were curious more than anything." Riley glanced at her husband. "Nothing like we're experiencing now. I'm not sure how useful that is, but there has to be some reason they've changed, some reason they're acting this way."

"Maybe it has to do with the bones," Brooke said. She looked up at Nat. "Do you think that could be it?"

"I don't know. Animals have a better sense of smell than we do, and it's possible they could have picked up on it." She hadn't considered a connection between the two, but what if the bones *hadn't* been in the crawl space while the Riordans were living there? "Do you have any idea how long the house was vacant before you bought it?"

"A couple of months, at least. They needed time to find a couple of suckers from out of town," Jason said. "No one from Longview would be stupid enough to buy it."

"Jason…" Riley placed a hand over his. "I'm really sorry. This is my fault."

"I'm not blaming you. Who in the hell could have predicted this? I mean, really. First Bigfoot, and now bones. Who would have believed it? Silver could have told you the straight-up truth, and we still would have bought the place. No one would have believed this craziness."

Nat hadn't met the real estate agent, but she imagined him explaining that there was at least one aggressive Sasquatch on the property, perhaps more. Would anyone have believed him? Anyone from outside Longview, that is?

The years spent hosting *Nat's Mysterious World* gave her the answer. "You aren't alone. There are people all over the world who would believe you," she said. "And I'm one of them."

CHAPTER EIGHTEEN

In the way of most things, it got worse before it got better.

The truth was straight out of Nat's nightmares. The bones *were* human bones, and worse, the bones of children. The skeletons of five children had been hidden in the Tanners' crawlspace. Because they'd been stripped of flesh and there was no trauma to the bones, it was impossible to tell how they had died.

Nat took care of Brooke while Riley and Jason were subjected to hours of grueling interrogations and polygraph tests, but in the end, another kind of test had saved them—forensic. The children had been dead long before the Tanners had moved to Longview. Though Jason's job gave him mobility and opportunity, the dates simply didn't match up. His alibis, provided by the trucking company, were sound.

It was a much sadder and wiser family that was finally allowed to return to the house at 1699 Forest Drive, trudging toward it like shell-shocked soldiers prepared to meet their doom. With all the recent turmoil, there had been no time or energy left to tackle the Sasquatch problem.

"If it makes you feel better, we couldn't find any evidence the house was ever a crime scene," one of the officers had said. "It was just a dumping ground."

It didn't make them feel better.

Riley appeared to take it astonishingly well when she saw what the cops had done to her lovely home, but Nat thought she glimpsed tears in the woman's eyes a few times. And who could blame her? The place had been torn apart. Even Brooke's room had been ransacked during the search for evidence. Nat understood the cops had been doing their jobs, but she hated them a little when she took in the extent of the destruction. Hadn't this poor family suffered enough? Thankfully, Jason's company had been unexpectedly understanding, and had given him some time off with pay. He didn't have to leave them for a few nights yet, which meant one less worry.

"Nothing a bit of elbow grease and some rock n' roll won't cure," he said when he surveyed the wreckage left behind. As he blasted classic rock on the stereo and spun his daughter around the kitchen, Riley smiled again. And Nat saw the Tanners were going to be okay. In spite of the fact they had to live in the Monster House.

After a full day of cleaning, the place looked noticeably better. It would never be quite the same, and the specter of the bones would probably always haunt them, but it was as close to good as it could possibly be.

As they shared a pepperoni-and-mushroom pizza, even Brooke looked exhausted.

"I was worried we'd have trouble sleeping here tonight, but I don't think that's going to be a problem." Riley ruffled her daughter's hair.

"Not for me." In the interlude spent at the inn, Nat had grown a lot stronger, and her wound had healed enough to remove the bandages. She had a wicked scar on her forehead that Brooke said reminded her of Harry Potter, but that didn't bother her much. She was old enough to know the deepest scars are the ones unseen. "I'm wiped."

Wiped, but inspired to tackle her own mess when she got home. *All* of the mess—the literal mess she'd left in her house, but also the mess of her life. It was time to get back in the game. She hadn't yet had the heart to break it to them that she was leaving, but she'd have to soon. It was high time for her to get on with her life and leave the Tanners to theirs. The house on Forest Drive felt different. In spite of her ghoulish find, she didn't feel anyone was in danger there anymore.

She couldn't have been more wrong.

* * *

Brooke tried to yell, but the hand pressed down on her mouth harder, smothering her cries.

When the strong arms carried her from the house, away from her family and Nat, she began to fight, but it was like she was a fly caught in a spider's web. The massive muscles of her captor pinned her arms to her side, so all she could do was flail her legs. She was so far off the ground, she was terrified the intruder would drop her.

Mom! Dad! She screamed in her mind. *Nat!* But the best she could manage was a muffled whimper. That would never wake them—they'd all been so tired. She hoped the police, the police that her parents suspected were still watching the house, would stop them and save her. But that was silly. What could the police possibly do? What could anyone do? She was going to die, and no one would ever understand what had happened to her.

She would be the new bones in the basement.

The thing carrying her howled, and the unexpected loudness of it made her cringe, and try harder to get away. Answering howls came from the forest, and she felt the creature's heart pounding hard against her shoulder.

Was this really happening?

Maybe she was having a nightmare, the granddaddy of all nightmares, where she could smell the animal's rank, musky odor and taste the blood in her mouth from where she'd bitten her tongue.

How long she was carried before the creature set her down, she didn't know. Seconds became minutes and minutes became hours. The moment her bare feet touched the ground, she broke into a sprint, but the creature dragged her back by her nightgown. Glaring at her with its yellow eyes, it shook its huge head. Brooke panted, struggling to catch a breath, positive she would die of fright.

No one could survive this, no one.

The creature grunted, a low, guttural sound that vibrated through her chest. It gestured behind her and she turned, terrified that a group of them would be standing in the forest, watching her.

To her shock, she saw her house. Though surrounded by trees, she had an unobstructed view of the back of the home.

And then she spotted something else.

She wanted to cry out, to warn them, but the hand pressed over her mouth again. Not as hard as before, but enough to stifle any sound. It shook its head at her once more, but its eyes no longer seemed as fierce.

Brooke watched in horror as the figure crept around the side of her house toward her window. She bit her lip to keep from screaming as he peered inside, obviously startled to find the screen had been removed.

That man had been coming for me. *He knows where my bedroom is.*

"He's going to hurt my family," she said to the creature, not knowing or caring if it understood her or not. She needed to warn them, to wake up the whole house. But the creature continued to hold her still, and shake its head.

After staring into the house for a few more minutes, as if willing Brooke to reappear, the man left, becoming another shadow among many.

Brooke crouched in the woods, frozen, unable to believe what she had seen. It was impossible to breathe, difficult to swallow. Her mouth was as dry as sandpaper. Finally, she found the nerve to look at the creature. It had crouched down too, and had a hold on her nightgown, but only with two fingers. In the meager light from the moon, it was difficult to make out much of its face beyond the hair that covered it and the enormous yellow eyes.

Seeing she was watching it, it let go of her nightgown and rustled in the leaves behind it. Brooke wasn't sure what to do. Should she try to run away again? Should she scream? But for some inexplicable reason, she wasn't as afraid of the creature any longer. She had a feeling it didn't want to harm her.

If it wanted to kill me, it would have already.

It turned back to her, something small clutched in one gigantic hand. Extending its arm toward her, it slowly uncurled its fingers.

She gasped. It was a skull, about the size of her own. Maybe a little smaller. Its empty eye sockets stared back at her, saying everything the creature couldn't.

She could have taken it as a threat, or a promise of things to come, but she knew the creature hadn't done this.

The man did.

She met the creature's glowing yellow eyes, and no longer saw them as angry or hateful.

Instead, they were full of sorrow. The creature was crying.

* * *

She awakened to the sound of her parents calling her.

Brooke sat up, setting off an avalanche of leaves. Panicking as she remembered what had happened, she scanned the forest for the creature, but it was gone.

It did what it had to do.

When had she fallen asleep? *How* had she fallen asleep? She couldn't recall, just had a vague memory of the creature not letting her return to the house.

Brooke yelped when she discovered the child's skull, resting on a pile of leaves beside her. The Sasquatch had left it for her, wanted her to have it.

How many kids have died in these woods?

Holding onto a tree, she used it to pull herself to a standing position. Reluctant to touch the skull, she picked it up anyway and held it to her chest. She knew from watching crime shows with her mom that the police could tell who this skull belonged to by studying the teeth. If she were lost in these woods, with her parents sad and worried, she'd want someone to find her. Someone to tell what had happened to her.

The man.

Best not to think about him. Not yet.

With twigs and rocks scratching the bottom of her feet, Brooke made her way out of the forest, squinting as she broke into the sun. They were so far away, too far away, but she could see them: her Mom, Dad, and Nat. Her dad was in the lead, holding a shotgun. Her mom was screaming for her.

"I'm here," Brooke, cried, relieved her voice still worked. "I'm over here."

Exhausted and trembling, she collapsed on the grass and waited to be rescued.

* * *

"We believe you, honey. Of course we do." Her mom hesitated. "But imagine how this would sound to someone who doesn't know you, or someone who doesn't understand what's been happening to us. Would you have believed your story before we moved here?"

Brooke cradled the skull on her lap. She could tell it made her parents uncomfortable, and her dad had suggested putting it somewhere else, but there was no way she was letting it go. It was her only proof of what had happened last night.

"But I'm telling the truth. You always said that as long as I told the truth, I would never have anything to worry about."

"Ordinarily that's true. But these are—" her mom paused, looking at Nat. "There are special circumstances."

Brooke looked at Nat too. "*You* wouldn't lie, would you?"

"For a good cause, I would. And right now, the most important thing is to get the police to believe your story. If they believe it, they'll protect you. And they'll catch the guy who was lurking around your window last night. Keeping you safe is all I care about."

"He's the killer. The guy who killed all those kids." Brooke stared at the skull in her hands, wondering who the little girl had been. For it was undoubtedly a little girl's skull—she was sure of it.

"Excuse me," her mom said, and left the room. Brooke knew she was crying. Her mom hated to cry in front of other people, but they could all see how scared she was. Her dad was scared too.

"You believe me, don't you?" she asked Nat, seeing storm clouds drift across her friend's face. What had happened to her was impossible for Nat to understand. The creatures had hurt her, cracked her skull. Animals like them had killed her friends.

But they had *saved* Brooke. The creature had taken her from her room to protect her, she was willing to bet on it.

"I do, but the police won't. Your parents are telling the truth. For just this one time, you're going to have to make up a story."

* * *

By the time the cops arrived, Brooke was well rehearsed. She had narrowly escaped from a man who'd climbed into her window the night before. She'd managed to slip his grasp and ran into her parents' room screaming. By the time the elder Tanners realized what was happening, the guy had taken off.

The officers took the skull from her, sealing it in a clear plastic bag.

"We didn't get a good look at him," Jason said, "but we'd sure like to."

"I understand. I have a daughter at home, and I'd feel the same way," said the officer, a kindly man with understanding brown eyes. "Don't worry. We'll have a few officers watching your house for the next few nights, and when he comes back, we'll grab him."

"What if he doesn't come back?"

"Then we'll find him somewhere else. But we will find him, Mr. Tanner."

"Good. A guy like that shouldn't be walking around free. Do you think he's responsible for the bones in our basement?"

"It's hard to say at this point," the officer said. "But if he isn't, it's one hell of a coincidence, and I don't believe in coincidences."

"I've never had much use for them either."

Why were they talking about this stuff that didn't matter? Brooke thought. Why were they acting like everything was fine? *Nothing* was fine. "How are you going to stop him from killing more kids?" she asked. She interrupted her dad, who'd been about to say something else dumb, but he was just going to have to forgive her.

"Now, we don't know for sure that the man who tried to kidnap you is the same one responsible for the murdered children," the officer said in a gentle voice. "I understand that what happened to you last night was really scary, but—"

"He's the same guy," Brooke protested, pointing at the skull. "He left that behind. It's from one of the victims." She ignored the shocked looks from Nat and her dad. If they wanted her to tell stories, she'd tell stories.

The cop looked over at the skull, shaking his head. Brooke could tell he was bothered by it—everyone was. What if the little girl, whoever she was, had died in those woods? What if she'd been killed not far from her house? What if she'd been so close, she'd been able to see Brooke's room when she died? "I'm sorry you're going through this," he said to her dad. "No family should have to go through what you have."

"Thank you," Brooke said.

The cop looked at her as if remembering that she was there, listening. "How old did you say you were again?"

"Ten." Brooke wondered what her age had to do with anything.

When her dad showed the officer to the door and they thought she couldn't hear, he asked the cop in a low voice if he *really* thought the man would come back.

"There's a chance. I'd say a good chance. You didn't catch him in the act, so as far as he's concerned, yesterday was bad timing. There's no reason for him not to make another attempt."

"I wish you'd let me take care of it."

Brooke had seen the rage on her dad's face that morning when she'd told him what had happened, and she had no doubt he would kill that man if given a chance.

"Sorry, sir—I understand the position you're in. As I said, I have daughters too. Trust us to handle this legally. I'll be back tonight with another officer. But…" he hesitated, "…if he comes back when we're not here, and you feel under threat…."

"Thank you, officer. I understand."

"I'm sure you do."

CHAPTER NINETEEN

It was enough to push her completely over the edge. She had someone in her sights who'd not only encountered a Sasquatch, but had gotten up close and personal with them. Brooke had lived to tell the tale, but to Nat's dismay, she didn't appear to be the slightest bit interested in talking about it.

"You weren't scared at all?" Nat pressed, knowing she should let it go. The kid, though she'd aged overnight, was only ten, and she'd been traumatized. No wonder she didn't feel like talking.

Brooke narrowed her eyes. "Of *course* I was scared…at first. Until I saw the man. When it showed me the man staring in my window, looking for me, I wasn't scared of the creature anymore. What if I'd been asleep, Nat? What if that guy had found me and taken me away?"

She didn't want to contemplate it. Thinking of all the young girls who'd been taken from their homes, never to return—or who were found after enduring unimaginable psychological and physical abuse—she hugged Brooke close. As she held her, she could feel the girl's shoulders shaking. It filled her with fury. Brooke was too young to have worries like this. "We would have gotten you back. But that's never going to happen. Don't worry."

Thanks to a creature she'd thought wanted to kill them, or at the very least, frighten them away. After she'd found the bones, no one had imagined the killer would still be hanging around the house. Had Brooke been his target all along?

"But what if he comes back when the police aren't here?" Brooke's face was unnaturally pale. Nat could see the faint red streaks her tears had left. "You and Mom and Dad can't watch me forever."

It was true. Brooke was too smart to believe a lie, or a flimsy platitude. If someone was obsessed enough, wanted something badly enough, he usually found a way to get it. There was no other option—the cops *had* to nab this guy, or he'd never give up. Other children's bones would end up in someone else's basement. She said the only thing she could think of that might bring the girl peace. "Then something else will be watching, as you found out last night."

"Do you think things will be different with the creatures now?"

"Probably. Once the cops catch this monster, there will be no reason for them to scare you away from the house. You'll likely never see them again."

It was so difficult for her to wrap her head around, but it made sense. The pounding on the window, tearing off the door—Nat suspected it had been a tactic to make the Tanners feel unsafe, to get them to leave the house.

Because they *hadn't* been safe, but not for the reason they'd thought.

"That's sad...that I'll never see them again." Brooke wiped her face with a tissue.

"I would have thought that's what you wanted. Do you really want them pounding on the window whenever you and your mom are trying to watch a movie?"

She sniffled. "I don't think it would be so scary anymore, now that I get what they were trying to do. I kind of like the idea that they were looking out for us whenever Dad was away."

The girl leaned her head against Nat's shoulder, and Nat put an arm around her. They sat that way for a long time. "Me too."

* * *

When the officer let down her hair, the plan became obvious. With her youthful face, she could easily pass for Brooke in the darkened bedroom. At least, long enough to fool a predator.

The woman was friendly. She smiled a lot and had a soft way of speaking. Brooke liked her. "Thanks for lending me your room," she said.

"No problem." Brooke would stay with Nat in the guestroom, and she was excited—it was kind of like a sleepover with a friend, something she hadn't had since they'd moved to Longview. "Are you scared?"

The cop winked at her. "Not a bit. *He's* the one who should be scared."

It took a week.

Nat exchanged a lot of concerned glances with her parents, none of them saying much. The mood in the house deteriorated. Her mom, not used to having her dad around so often, began to snap at him. Her dad retreated to the shed, spending long hours working on "projects" that never amounted to anything.

What if he had to go back to work before the man returned, leaving them alone? And what about the police? They couldn't stay there forever. They had other cases to solve, other people who needed them.

What if they got sick of waiting for the man and left before he came back? What if the three of them had to fight him on their own? With so many people around, the creatures hadn't been sighted since the night Brooke had been taken from her bedroom. She worried they were gone.

Another worry kept her awake at night, staring at the ceiling. Nat would be going home soon. Brooke could tell she'd stayed longer than she'd wanted to, longer than she'd intended, just to make sure the Tanners were all right. But she'd come to Longview to fight the creature. That wasn't necessary anymore. Brooke's parents may not have been one-hundred percent positive of the creatures' intent, but she was. She'd never forget the way it had cradled the child's skull in its huge hands, the sadness in its eyes. It had been putting on its ferocious act to warn them, to scare them away before something terrible happened.

Brooke didn't want Nat to leave. The woman was her only friend, the one person she could be completely honest with, the one who understood her the most. Though Nat's experience with creatures had been very different from Brooke's, they were among the few people in the world who had been close enough to touch them, to hear them breathe.

Shouts from her room made her sit up fast, her eyes wide as she strained to see in the dark. She couldn't make out what the adults were saying—the words were coming too fast—but she knew what it meant.

The man was back.

Remembering the aura of evil that had surrounded the figure lurking around her house, peering in her window, she shrank under the covers and prayed the officers wouldn't let him get away.

* * *

In Brooke's room, chaos reigned.

Officer Mansfield had the presence of mind to wait until the man climbed in the window, rendering a speedy escape unlikely. As he eased the blankets off her and put his hand across her mouth, she pointed her gun at his face.

Seeing he'd been duped, the man sprang for the open window quicker than Mansfield would have thought possible. He was built like a human spider—all long, skinny limbs. Her own legs briefly tangled in the blankets, but she kicked herself free in time to grab him by the belt loop. He ripped away from her grasp and flung his body outside onto the grass.

She yelled for her partner as she clambered out the window after her quarry, and soon both of them were in pursuit, her partner easily catching up to her and staying slightly ahead.

They were no match for the fastest man they'd ever encountered, who bounded away from them as if he'd trained for the Olympics and this was merely a warm up.

"Stop, police," her partner bellowed, his voice cutting through the night air. She was grateful he had the wind; she needed all of hers for running. "Stop, or I'll shoot!" Desperation contorted his features. "Shit, he's getting away."

She saw that he was right. Though both in decent physical condition—her partner more than decent—they weren't running for their lives, and the man they were chasing was. That alone gave him an advantage.

As the man reached the tree line of the surrounding woods, Mansfield was overwhelmed with despair. If he got away, more children would die. More children would die because of *her*. Why hadn't she waited until he'd tried to pick her up? Why hadn't she blocked the window? Why hadn't she shot him? Yes, the paperwork and reprimands would have been a bitch, but it would have been worth it to know this guy was no longer terrorizing Longview, or anywhere else. Now a monster would be free and it was her fault.

Evidently not plagued by guilt, her partner picked up speed and plunged into the woods after the man, but this was the murderer's terrain. He'd no doubt stalked the Tanners with the help of that forest—the girl had mentioned how good a view she'd had of her house from there. What hope did they have? Still, she shook off the negative thoughts that threatened to turn her legs to stone, and took off after them.

She hadn't gone far before she heard her partner holler, but not in triumph.

Something had scared him. Badly.

I'll kill that son of a bitch if he's hurt him.

Discovering reserves she hadn't known existed, Mansfield ran faster than she had in her life, leaping over fallen branches and other obstacles like they were hurdles. She was going so fast she nearly ran smack into the back of her partner.

He was staring at something on the ground.

Relieved to see he wasn't hurt, she couldn't understand why he'd stopped. What in the hell was going on?

He turned to her, and then, with one of the strangest expressions she'd ever seen, engaged the flashlight on his phone to show her what had startled him so much.

It was the man, his neck tilted at an unnatural angle.

He was a grotesque ragdoll, lying across their path with his legs and arms in a tangle, as if a giant had simply picked him up and thrown him there, dashing him to the ground.

The chase was over.

EPILOGUE

"You decided to stay."

Riley recoiled, her fingers tightening on the grocery cart handle. She was always functioning on a hair trigger these days, but if that was the worst of her problems, she considered herself lucky.

She whirled to see a hostile-looking girl a few years older than her daughter. The girl towered over her, with a bizarre look on her face. It took Riley some time to understand that this was Clara's version of a smile.

"I'm glad. Someone had to stop that guy."

That guy had been the Riordan's nephew. Beth had confided that her nephew had always had disturbing, anti-social tendencies, but that she and Franklin had felt sorry for him. They'd thought some country air would do their nephew good, but their troubles with the creatures had begun soon afterwards, and when Mark had left without saying goodbye, it hadn't seemed unusual. He'd done the same before, many times, and by then, they were too consumed by what was happening around their home to give it much thought.

Learning their ne'er-do-well black sheep was a serial killer was almost too much for Beth to handle, but with time and the support of a good therapist, she'd started to recover. The Tanners and the Riordans kept in regular contact, speaking often, though Franklin was never going to be Jason's favorite person and Riley suspected vice versa. The two families were bonded forever now—bound together by tragedy, terror, and the fact that they were the only people in the world who knew what had stopped Mark Riordan for good.

Who else would believe them?

Something in the way Clara said "that guy" gave Riley chills. "Did you know him?"

She rolled her eyes. "Yeah, all the girls knew him. He tried to mess with me once, but he got what was coming to him." She brandished a massive fist. "He wasn't expecting that."

"I'm so relieved you weren't hurt. But if all the girls knew, why wasn't something done sooner? Why wasn't he arrested?"

"Because we're kids. Most of 'em were too damn scared to say a thing—Riordan had them right where he wanted 'em. He used fear to keep them quiet. And me? No one believes *me*. I've been telling people about this for years. No one ever listens to me."

Riley couldn't imagine what would have happened if Mark had succeeded in kidnapping her daughter. Brooke was a fighter too, but she was only ten years old, and slight. He would have quickly overpowered her.

But that didn't bear thinking about.

She had Brooke enrolled in Muay Thai classes, though Jason teased her that this was a case of "shutting the barn door after the horse has escaped." But he'd stopped laughing fast when she'd asked him if he really thought Mark Riordan was the lone monster Brooke would face during her life.

Clara leaned in, putting her big face too close to Riley's. "*They* caught 'im, didn't they?"

Ordinarily, she'd have played dumb. She had that act down to a science. But this odd girl had told her the truth once, and Riley wasn't about to lie to her now. "Yes, I think they did."

She nodded, looking triumphant. "I *knew* it. They're nothing for us to be scared of, you know. They're not mean. They stay out of our way, as much as they can. But they can't stand seeing children hurt. I thought something like this would happen a long time ago. That Riordan guy sure picked the wrong house."

"How do you know so much about them?" Other shoppers squeezed to get past them in the narrow aisle, but Riley didn't care if they overheard. How did this girl understand what everyone else had missed?

Clara shrugged. "I dunno. Common sense, I guess. If they wanted to hurt us, they would have long before now."

She sauntered down the aisle, away from Riley, pushing past the other shoppers, ignoring their frowns and muttered epithets.

. She'd said her piece, and now she could move on. Riley doubted the girl would speak to her about it again.

"Now you know who the monster was," Clara said, and left.

* * *

"Welcome to *Nat's Mysterious World.* I'm your host, Nat McPherson, and you're either a twisted individual or seriously in need of a hobby."

It felt uncomfortable, but in a good way. She'd made peace with discomfort lately, understanding that getting comfortable with being uncomfortable was the key to regaining her life.

Facing her creditors had been uncomfortable.

Telling her therapist how she actually felt about Andrew's death had been uncomfortable.

Cleaning her place of accumulated filth and joining AA had been uncomfortable. And the first meeting? Ugh. But now she found she kind of looked forward to them. Almost.

This latest step back to herself—returning to work—was her final step, or so she hoped. Choosing the first guest of the new-and-improved *Nat's Mysterious World* had been a no-brainer.

"We've got a special treat for you tonight. Not only is she the youngest guest we've ever had on the cast, she's the one person who can say she was saved by a Sasquatch. Welcome, Brooke Tanner."

"Thanks for having me on the show," Brooke said, sounding years older than her age. Some things never changed.

"Thanks for being here. Our listeners aren't aware of this yet, but we share an unusual bond. The creature that saved *you* nearly killed *me.*"

"Because it was scared," Brooke said. "It thought you were dangerous."

"Wise creature. I *am* dangerous." Nat laughed for the sake of her audience, but the girl's insistence that the creatures were harmless disturbed her. It was more complicated than that. She was willing to bet they hadn't been threatened by her in the slightest. They'd had another reason for gifting her with a cracked skull and daily headaches.

A reason that didn't bear thinking about too closely.

She thought of the last photo Igor had texted her. The Russian doctors had done the best job they could reconstructing his face, but no one was going to mistake him for a supermodel.

At night, when she was alone in her silent house, her thoughts were even more disturbing. What had happened to Andrew—to Steven—and to the others played over and over in her mind like a gruesome creature feature she would never finish, reminding her why she'd started drinking in the first place.

These days, she called her sponsor instead.

"Do you still see it?" she asked Brooke, knowing she should start with the family's story first, but not able to wait that long.

"No, not since…the last time. But I know it's there," the girl said.

"I can feel it watching me."

THE END

ACKNOWLEDGMENTS

Thanks to the team at Severed Press for their hard work and commitment to these crazy creature features, and a special thank you to Hunter Shea for the amazing blurb.

To all the readers and friends who continue to encourage my crazy writing dreams, I can't imagine doing this without you: Christine Brandt, Simon Fuller, Kimberly Yerina, Nikki Burch, Andy Mondaca and Rhonda Sandberg, Tara Clark, Jocelyn Boileau, Catherine Cavendish, Dana Krawchuk, R.J. Crowther Jr. from Mysterious Galaxy, John Toews from McNally Robinson Booksellers, Janine Pipe, Steve Stredulinsky, Erik Smith, Hunter Shea, JG Faherty, Teel James Glenn, Henry Harner, Wai Chan, Jim Edwards, Lee Murray, Lisa Saunders, Wil Ralston, Chris Brogden, and the wonderful Insecure Writers Support Group.

With love to all of my students—past, present, and future. You keep me going.

Check out other great
Cryptid Novels!

J.H. Moncrieff
RETURN TO DYATLOV PASS

In 1959, nine Russian students set off on a skiing expedition in the Ural Mountains. Their mutilated bodies were discovered weeks later. Their bizarre and unexplained deaths are one of the most enduring true mysteries of our time. Nearly sixty years later, podcast host Nat McPherson ventures into the same mountains with her team, determined to finally solve the mystery of the Dyatlov Pass incident. Her plans are thwarted on the first night, when two trackers from her group are brutally slaughtered. The team's guide, a superstitious man from a neighboring village, blames the killings on yetis, but no one believes him. As members of Nat's team die one by one, she must figure out if there's a murderer in their midst—or something even worse—before history repeats itself and her group becomes another casualty of the infamous Dead Mountain.

Gerry Griffiths
CRYPTID ZOO

As a child, rare and unusual animals, especially cryptid creatures, always fascinated Carter Wilde. Now that he's an eccentric billionaire and runs the largest conglomerate of high-tech companies all over the world, he can finally achieve his wildest dream of building the most incredible theme park ever conceived on the planet... CRYPTID ZOO. Even though there have been apparent problems with the project, Wilde still decides to send some of his marketing employees and their families on a forced vacation to assess the theme park in preparation for Opening Day. Nick Wells and his family are some of those chosen and are about to embark on what will become the most terror-filled weekend of their lives—praying they survive. STEP RIGHT UP AND GET YOUR FREE PASS... TO CRYPTID ZOO

Check out other great

Cryptid Novels!

P.K. Hawkins

THE CRYPTID FILES

Fresh out of the academy with top marks, Agent Bradley Tennyson is expecting to have the pick of cases and investigations throughout the country. So he's shocked when instead he is assigned as the new partner to "The Crag," an agent well past his prime. He thinks the assignment is a punishment. It's anything but.Agent George Crag has been doing this job for far longer than most, and he knows what skeletons his bosses have in the closet and where the bodies are buried. He has pretty much free reign to pick his cases, and he knows exactly which one he wants to use to break in his new young partner: the disappearance and murder of a couple of college kids in a remote mountain town.Tennyson doesn't realize it, but Crag is about to introduce him to a world he never believed existed: The Cryptid Files, a world of strange monsters roaming in the night. Because these murders have been going on for a long time, and evidence is mounting that the murderer may just in fact be the legendary Bigfoot.

Gerry Griffiths

DOWN FROM BEAST MOUNTAIN

A beast with a grudge has come down from the mountain to terrorize the townsfolk of Porterville. The once sleepy town is suddenly wide awake. Sheriff Abel McGuire and game warden Grant Tanner frantically investigate one brutal slaying after another as they follow the blood trail they hope will eventually lead to the monstrous killer. But they better hurry and stop the carnage before the census taker has to come out and change the population sign on the edge of town to ZERO.

Check out other great
Cryptid Novels!

Hunter Shea
LOCH NESS REVENGE

Deep in the murky waters of Loch Ness, the creature known as Nessie has returned. Twins Natalie and Austin McQueen watched in horror as their parents were devoured by the world's most infamous lake monster. Two decades later, it's their turn to hunt the legend. But what lurks in the Loch is not what they expected. Nessie is devouring everything in and around the Loch, and it's not alone. Hell has come to the Scottish Highlands. In a fierce battle between man and monster, the world may never be the same. Praise for THEY RISE : "Outrageous, balls to the wall...made me yearn for 3D glasses and a tub of popcorn, extra butter!" – The Eyes of Madness "A fast-paced, gore-heavy splatter fest of sharksploitation." The Werd "A rocket paced horror story. I enjoyed the hell out of this book." Shotgun Logic Reviews

C.G. Mosley
BAKER COUNTY
BIGFOOT CHRONICLE

Marie Bledsoe only wants her missing brother Kurt back. She'll stop at nothing to make it happen and, with the help of Kurt's friend Tony, along with Sheriff Ray Cochran, Marie embarks on a terrifying journey deep into the belly of the mysterious Walker Laboratory to find him. However, what she and her companions find lurking in the laboratory basement is beyond comprehension. There are cryptids from the forest being held captive there and something...else. Enjoy this suspenseful tale from the mind of C.G. Mosley, author of Wood Ape. Welcome back to Baker County, a place where monsters do lurk in the night!

Printed in Great Britain
by Amazon

23230099R00098